FIREBALLS FROM HELL

Also by Rose Impey

The Girls' Gang

FIREBALLS FROM HELL

ROSE IMPEY

With illustrations by Colin Meir

Collins
An Imprint of HarperCollinsPublishers

First published in Great Britain by Collins in 1996
Collins is an imprint of
HarperCollins*Publishers* Ltd,
77-85 Fulham Palace Road,
Hammersmith, London W6 8JB

3 5 7 9 8 6 4

ISBN 0 00 674538 5

The author asserts the moral right to be
identified as the author of the work.

Printed and bound in Great Britain by
Caledonian International Book Manufacturing Ltd, Glasgow

To Sam for the ideas
and
Sue for the support

CHAPTER ONE

"Now, firstly, Sam . . . It's OK to call you Sam?"
Sam asked himself in a soft, confidential voice.
He imagined a glamorous reporter.

He smiled and shrugged, as if to say, feel free.

"OK, Sam . . . would you say you were a super-stitious person? Do you own any lucky charms?"

"Oh, sure," said Sam, deepening his voice for
effect. "I wouldn't go anywhere without my
lucky shark's tooth." Sam stroked the smooth,
sharp tooth he wore on a string round his neck. It
was, in fact, a dog's tooth, but it looked convinc-
ing.

*"Now, Sam, can you tell our readers how it's
changed you, becoming so famous?"*

Sam thought about this one and decided on modesty. "Not a bit," he said coolly. "I'm still just an ordinary fella. 'Course you get recognized wherever you go, but you learn to live with that."

"You must get lots of fan mail."

"Yeah, tons. And I read it all myself." Sam added hastily, "I think I owe that to my fans."

"So, erm, how do you explain your band's spectacular success?"

Sam grinned. This was his favourite question. "I think that's down to my personality," he said, this time abandoning all modesty. "I've always been a bit out of the ordinary . . ." Sam puffed himself up, "a bit of a hero-figure really . . ." he stuck his chest out, manfully, "a bit of a born leader . . ."

"A bit of a flaming poser," said his dad, putting his face round the door. "What on earth are you doing?"

Sam was so startled he dropped the torch which he was improvising as a microphone and it rolled under the bed. He leant over to retrieve it. "What does it look as if I'm doing? I'm practising being interviewed."

"Who'd want to interview you?"

"Smash Hits, Just Seventeen, Big. When we get to Number One, they'll all be queuing up. You

ought to think about getting another phone line in, we're going to need it."

Sam's dad looked at him as if he'd newly arrived from another planet. Sam picked up his mike.

"Look, I'm busy right now, Dad. Can you close the door on your way out?"

Sam's dad went downstairs shaking his head, muttering to himself, "He's unbelievable. The boy's unbelievable."

Luke sat in his garden shed, reading a pile of *Beano*s, with two lizards on his knee. He called the lizards Con and Dom, a joke his mum had not appreciated.

At first, he'd had to turn the lizards over to tell which was which – Con had a small black spot on his stomach. But then Dom lost his tail. Well, he hadn't exactly lost it, he'd shed it when Luke grabbed it by mistake, but it was beginning to grow back.

Luke's peace was interrupted by the shed door-handle rattling.

"What the flop do *you* want?" Luke shouted rudely.

"What're you doing in there?" his sister shouted back.

"Smoking." Luke liked to wind her up.

"I'm telling our mum."

"And drinking."

"You wouldn't dare . . ."

"And planning a murder."

"Whose?" said Lucy.

"Yours," said Luke. "Now clear off."

Lucy rattled the door-handle again. "Mum wants you to do a job."

"I'm doing a job. I'm doing my animals."

"You've been doing them all morning."

"Yes, well, there's a lot of them." At the last count, Luke's menagerie totalled 42: 2 lizards, 4 terrapins, 27 pigeons, 2 barn owls, a cockatiel and half a dozen rats.

"Now clear off or I'll let the rats out." And to show her he meant it, he rattled the cages. "Out you come, Wilbur," he said. "Templeton, come away from that door. You know Lucy doesn't want to play with you." Before he could mention Charlotte, Lucy was half-way down the garden path. A few weeks ago Luke had put Wilbur, his biggest rat, in Lucy's bed – she wasn't in it at the time, of course – and nearly frightened her to death. The shed was one place where he could get away from her.

Several comics later, the shed door-handle rattled again.

"What d'you want now, you little insect?" Luke called out.

"Oh, that's very nice," came a familiar voice.

Luke unlocked the door and let Sam in. Sam reeled back. "Aww, man, how can you stand it in there? It stinks."

Luke, embarrassed, followed him out. "I hardly notice it." The tell-tale blush spread over Luke's face until he looked like a bad case of sunburn.

"Are you gonna do that when we get on *Top of the Pops*?"

"Do what?"

"That impression of a boiled beetroot."

"What're you talking about?"

"I'm talking about *Our Band*!"

"Our *what*?"

"Come on," said Sam, leading Luke by the collar. "I'll tell you on the way to Jacko's."

Jamie sat in front of his computer screen, zapping small green aliens, his face a picture of concentration: "Pow! Pow! *POW!*" He sounded as if he was gargling.

"It can't do you any good sitting hour after hour in front of that screen," said his mum, coming in with an armful of clean clothes. "Why don't you go out for a bit of exercise. Get some fresh air."

"P-lease." Jamie went to great lengths to avoid exercise. He got more fresh air than he wanted just walking to school and back.

"But you haven't been out all weekend."

"I don't want to go out. It's cold."

"Jamie, it's April. The sun's shining."

"You know I don't like the sun. Makes me itch."

"It does not make you itch. Sunshine's good for you."

"Used to be, Mum. Used to be. Haven't you heard about the ozone layer?"

His mum sighed and went out, temporarily defeated. But she'd broken his concentration.

Jamie switched discs and called up the menu. He scanned the screen until he found his epic story: *The Adventures of Bert Lurch-Hooter, Master Spy and Private Detective*.

At the end of Chapter Five, Bert had stumbled on his old enemy The Big Boss Man and his partners in crime, Ghoul and the Weasel. They were up to their tricks again, smuggling in millions of pounds' worth of pirate video games. Bert had finally tracked them down to their hideaway in the cliffs on the coast of Kent. But, before he could alert his friend Inspector Crouch, the grotesque Ghoul and his seedy side-kick had caught Bert. Now he was nailed inside a crate which they were about to dump into the sea.

Jamie read the last line and smiled.

How will the brilliant Bert escape?

Jamie typed in, 'Chapter Six'.

Above all, Bert told himself, he must keep a clear head . . .

"Jamie," his mum shouted, "Luke and Sam are at the door."

Jamie didn't even look up. "Tell them to go away."

"They want to know if you're coming out."

"No."

"Oh, sweetheart. Why don't you go out with your friends . . ."

"Too busy."

"Too busy for your friends?"

Jamie sighed heavily. "All right, all right. Anything for a bit of peace." He turned off his computer and went out.

Sam and Luke were waiting on his doorstep,

grinning and nudging each other. Something was going on, but whatever it was, Jamie wasn't going to ask.

The boys walked down the road, three abreast.

"What've you been doing?" Sam asked.

Jamie shrugged. "Nothing. What about you?"

Sam looked sideways at Luke and they started smirking again.

Jamie fiddled with his earring and pretended not to notice.

"Tell him," Luke said to Sam.

"No. You tell him." Sam looked quite coy.

"It was your idea," Luke insisted.

Jamie let out a heavy breath. He just wished they'd get on with it. Sam opened his mouth to speak but Luke waved his hands wildly. "No. Show him."

The two boys grinned and stopped in the middle of the pavement. Jamie turned to face them. Sam slowly began to unzip his jacket, a ridiculous smile on his face. "Da, da, daaa, dadada daaaaaa . . ." he sang and wiggled his hips and stuck out his bottom.

Luke's face was on fire. Jamie dreaded to think what was coming. When Sam finally unveiled his T-shirt it was covered with luminous felt-pen letters, graffiti-style. It read, *Fireballs From Hell*.

"What d'you think?" said Sam, rolling his eyes and grinning. "Awesome, or what?"

CHAPTER TWO

"It'd look better on the side of the co-op," spluttered Jamie.

"Excuse me, but was that a joke?" said Sam.

"Well, Fireballs from Hell! What's it supposed to be?"

"It's the name of our band," Sam almost snarled.

"Whose band?"

"The band we're gonna start." This sounded as if it should be accompanied by a drum roll.

Jamie looked at Luke who nodded excitedly. "You wanna be in it, don't you?"

Jamie raised his eyebrows. "For a start, I can't

play anything." He was kind enough not to add, and neither can you two.

"You could sing," Luke suggested.

"You've heard me sing."

"We'll find you a job," said Sam.

"What sort of job?"

"Roadie."

Luke burst out laughing. "He's a bit small, isn't he?"

"We'll buy him a grow-bag for Christmas."

Jamie ignored this. "What would I have to do?"

"Load and unload the equipment. Set it up. Keep any yobs off the stage."

"Not girls," added Luke. "We don't mind them mobbing us."

"Just heavies," Sam agreed.

Luke looked Jamie up and down. "I don't know about a grow-bag, he'll need a body transplant."

"Look here, Beanpole," said Jamie.

"Now, guys!" Sam held each one by the shoulder. "We haven't got time to be scrapping. We've got to get this band on the road. We've got a demo tape to make."

Luke and Jamie looked at Sam in disbelief.

"That's what you have to do, to enter the

competition. Look." Sam whipped a copy of *Smash Hits* out of his jacket pocket. "You send a stamped addressed envelope for the entrance form – which I've done, so you owe me for the stamps – then we send photos and a demo tape. If we get into the last three we get a promo video made and the chance of a record contract with Mega Records."

"You didn't tell me any of this," said Luke.

"I'm telling you now, aren't I?"

"You've already entered us?" said Jamie, incredulous.

"I've sent off for a form! We've nothing to lose. They're looking for new young bands, like us. Undiscovered talent."

"What do they mean by young? How young?" said Jamie, grabbing the magazine off Sam and studying the small print. "You're supposed to be fourteen!"

Sam waved his hands as if this was a mere detail. "Look, Pea Brain, if we send in the best demo tape they won't care if we're still in nappies. Trust me, this could be our big chance."

Sam looked at Jamie, who was shaking his head, and Luke, who was already worrying about whether it was going to cost him anything. Sometimes they were a real disappointment to him.

"At least try and look excited, you pair of earwigs."

The boys walked on for a while in silence. When they reached the shops, Sam sat down on the wall outside the video shop.

"What we need is a list." Sam's lists were legendary. Whatever Sam was engaged in, whatever obsessive new scheme he was working on, it always started with a list. "Give us a pen."

The two boys searched their pockets. Pen and paper were not regulation equipment for Luke or Sam, but Jamie, as a budding novelist, always carried a notebook. He opened it on a clean page and tried to hand it over to Sam, but Sam waved it away.

"You write," he said.

Jamie sat down on the pavement, with his back to the wall. "Go on, then," he said.

"OK," said Sam, "What do we need?"

"Instruments?"

"We've got instruments." He nodded towards Luke. "Me and Lulu've got guitars."

"How about instruments you can play?"

"What d'you mean? We're learning, aren't we? Luke's having lessons. I can play a few chords."

19

"But we can't make a band out of two guitars," said Luke.

"And a roadie," said Jamie.

"Half a roadie," Luke corrected him.

"Knock it off." Jamie flung the notebook into the air.

Sam got up and retrieved it; he gave Luke a silent warning.

Jamie was understandably sensitive about his height. He was the smallest boy in their class. Even most of the girls were taller than him. Going around with Sam and Luke didn't help. Sam was big, in every sense, the biggest boy in the class. And Luke *was* like a beanpole, thin and stringy with big ears. He was sometimes nicknamed Handles.

"Sorry, sorry, sorry," said Luke.

Jamie tried to ignore them, but Sam handed the notebook back, smiling winningly at him. Jamie curled his lip and snatched hold of the book.

"OK. Number one: more instruments," said Sam, recapping.

"Two: people to play them," said Luke.

"Yeah. Yeah."

"Three: somewhere to meet and practise," said Jamie.

"Right," said Sam. "And four: transport."

"Transport?"

"To *transport* our equipment."

Jamie and Luke looked at Sam. "Equipment?"

"Amplifiers and things." Both boys looked back doubtfully. "OK. Five: money to buy equipment," he conceded.

"Six: dancers," said Luke.

Jamie snorted.

"Just write it down," said Sam. "Then if we get through we're gonna need the gear."

"Gear?" said Jamie.

"Designer clothes, you dodo," said Luke.

"Photographic sessions," said Sam.

"Image consultants," said Luke.

"Accountants."

"A stretch limo . . ."

"Private jet . . ."

Jamie had stopped writing way back. He stared at them, wondering what planet they were on. He waited until they ran out of steam. "Is that it?" he enquired. "I mean, can we stop and bring a bit of common sense to this conversation before it self-ignites and disappears into the stratosphere. Where do you two spanners think we're going to get amplifiers from, or for that matter a transit van, never mind the fact none of us can drive.

You need money for that kind of thing. And lots of it."

"Don't look at me," said Luke hastily. Money was always a sore point with him. Everything he really wanted to do seemed to depend on it.

But nothing phased Sam. "It's cool," he said. "We'll get it."

"How?"

"We'll earn it."

"Have you forgotten school starts back tomorrow?" said Jamie.

"Oh, cheer us up, why don't you," said Luke.

Any thought of school was enough to dampen their spirits, but not knowing who'd be teaching them made the prospect even worse. Their regular teacher, Mr Harrison, otherwise known as Hazza or The Foghorn, was going to be on a course for the next month.

"Who do you think we'll get?" asked Sam.

"Cod Liver Oil," said Jamie, with glee.

"The Suit?" said Luke. They all thought this was unlikely. Mr Burton, the Headteacher, was far too busy. "Perhaps we'll have the Catacombs?"

Jamie put two fingers down his throat and mimed being horribly sick. "We don't want her. The old carthorse."

22

"Anyway, makes no odds," said Sam. "We've got more important things to think about. We've got this band to run."

At best, school was an obstacle to the boys' plans, or it would have been, if they'd let it. But with years of practice they were skilled at adapting the school day to their own ends, their latest hobby and current obsession. This term it would be *The Band*.

The boys slowly made their way back home, dropping Jamie off first at the end of his road.

"See you at school, then, you pair of weevils," he called back.

"Not if we see you first, Amoeba Brain," shouted Sam.

Luke and Sam walked on towards the railbridge.

"D'you suppose amoeba have brains?" asked Luke.

"Yeah," said Sam. "Probably the same size as Jacko's."

Both boys thought about this for a moment.

"No," they said together. "Bigger. Definitely bigger."

CHAPTER THREE

It was eight o'clock. Sam's dad came in from the yard for his breakfast.

"Where's Superstar?" he asked.

Sam's mum smiled and pointed upstairs.

"It's time he was up. He's turning into one of those teenage layabouts."

"Oh, leave him alone," said his mum. "He'll grow out of it."

"It's no wonder he's getting fat. Laying about, talking to himself."

"He's not fat. He's going to be a big boy."

"Big girl, you mean. He spends more time in front of a mirror than any girl I ever knew."

Sam's mum finished cleaning up the baby and

sat Ruby on the rug with a biscuit in her hand.

"Boys are like that nowadays."

Sam's dad snorted. He spent most of his time in a pair of overalls, under the bonnet of a car. You wouldn't catch him standing in front of a mirror talking to himself.

"Have you listened to him?"

"No, I haven't." Sam's mum gave riding lessons. With four children and four horses she was too busy to hang around eavesdropping at her son's bedroom door.

Sam's dad went to the bottom of the stairs. "He's at it now. I bet he's on about that band again."

"Oh, don't go winding him up before he goes to school."

But Sam's dad grinned and waved her words away. Carrying his mug he silently climbed the stairs.

Sam was studying the list, frowning, and talking to himself. "More instruments," he read. "Pass. People to play them. Hmmm. Somewhere to practise. Easy." That was one he'd worked out. "Transport. Equipment. Money. Yeah, yeah, yeah." Sam folded up the list. No point depressing himself completely. He'd got school this morning.

"Can you think of any advice you'd give other people just starting up?" Sam asked himself into the mike. *"Other young groups struggling to get going?"*

"My motto has always been: Never give up," he said, with conviction. "You've gotta have confidence in yourself. You've gotta make it happen. You've gotta keep in there. When the going gets tough – the tough get going."

Sam's dad stood outside the door, silently shaking with laughter.

"Iron will. That's what you need." Sam tightened his fist and stuck out his chin.

As his dad bent forward to hear the next hilarious instalment, Sam opened his bedroom door, almost knocking his dad over.

"Ah, Dad! Just the person I wanted to see. I need a favour – it's no big deal. Honest, Dad, all I want . . ."

But Sam's dad was gone before Sam could finish his sentence.

Luke was still in bed, with the quilt up to his chin. His sister Lucy had been into his room three times already.

"You're going to be late for school."

"It's the first day back, you know."

"Mum says you've got to get up *this instant*!"

Each time she grew more frantic, as if someone was winding her up like a clockwork toy.

Luke's mum had called him a couple of times too. "Luke, have you seen the time?"

"He hasn't moved, Mum," Lucy shrieked. "He's not even dressed yet."

Lucy was quite prepared to risk being late herself in order to keep up a running commentary on her brother's lack of movement.

"Luke, I won't tell you again," his mum called up.

"He's *still* in bed," Lucy squealed.

It was half-past eight. Lucy felt triumphant. She was hopping around the upstairs landing, waiting for justice to descend on Luke. When she heard their mum's footsteps coming up the stairs Lucy darted into Luke's room.

"Now you're going to get it. Oh, boy, are you going to get it."

"Don't wet yourself," said Luke, perfectly calmly.

He lay there another moment. Then, just as their mum reached the top step, he threw back his quilt and stood up, revealing himself fully dressed, with his school bag ready packed over his shoulder.

Luke tossed his quilt neatly back across his bed and walked out to meet his mum.

"I didn't want any breakfast; I've got a Snicker in my bag." He turned to Lucy. "Have a nice day," he said.

Lucy deflated like a balloon blown up to the point of bursting and then released to fly round the room squeaking and shrieking until all that's left is a shrivelled scrap of rubber. Her screams followed Luke out of the house and down the road. *"I HATE HIM!"*

Jamie stood over his mum and supervised the making of his packed lunch. His sandwiches, white and crustless, sat ready on the worktop. He curled back the edges and inspected the contents.

"Ham," said his mum.

"Just checking."

Jamie only ate two things: ham sandwiches and cheese sandwiches.

"Don't you ever fancy a change?"

"Nope."

"It's not what you'd call a balanced diet." His mum was always on to Jamie about eating fruit or vegetables, something fresh. But when she suggested it, Jamie looked at her as if she'd asked him to eat mouse droppings or frog spawn or something.

"Mum, have you got a decent photo I could have?"

"Who of?"

"Me, of course." Who else would he want a photograph of?

"Probably. They'll be in the drawer."

Jamie went off to look. He came back with a couple.

"I look about eight in these." He showed them to his mum.

"That's because you were eight."

"Haven't we got something more recent?"

"If you tell me what it's for . . ."

"Oh, nothing," he said, evasively. "Probably won't happen. Some daft idea of Spam's. Just something and nothing. Nothing really . . ." he trailed off.

"Well, that's much clearer," said his mum.

Luke walked towards the school gates in high spirits. Fresh from his victory over Public Enemy Number One and thinking about his future as a pop idol, he smiled at everyone he passed. But when he saw Sam and Jamie waiting for him, he could tell they didn't share his rosy view of the world.

"What's up with you pair?"

"Tell him," said Sam.

"You tell him," said Jamie.

"Oh, don't start that. What is it?"

Sam looked at Jamie and rolled his eyes. "D'you want the good news or the bad news?"

Luke groaned. "Let's have the bad news."

"Guess who we've got," said Jamie. He did an imitation of a heavy horse cantering.

"The Catacombs?" shrieked Luke. "Aw, man, she only takes infants."

"Not any more," said Sam.

Suddenly Luke's good mood evaporated into thin air. The school bell rang and the boys dragged themselves into the cloakroom.

"Look. Concentrate on the positive," said Sam. "We've got the band. There's nothing The Carthorse can do about that."

Luke wasn't convinced. "Anyway, what was the good news?" he asked, looking for some crumb of comfort.

"Victoria Topping broke her arm."

"Just her arm?" said Luke, disappointed.

CHAPTER FOUR

Mrs Carter-Coombes, the vicar's wife, was one of the regular supply teachers for the infant department. Most of the class had been taught by her in their early school-days, so they were all careful not to laugh when she said, "And when you've finished your writing and done a little picture to go with it, you can put your books away." All except Billy Brewer, who whispered, too loudly, ". . . in your little drawers."

Two fingers took hold of his ear and tweaked it until he rose, as if levitating, out of his seat.

"We may think we're a big boy but we still have a few lessons to learn, don't we, Billy?" said Mrs Carter-Coombes.

Billy sank back into his seat and rubbed his ear. It was all over in seconds but it was a useful reminder of the infamous fingers.

"Come back, Mr Harrison, all is forgiven," whispered Sam.

The teacher flashed a look at Sam. "I've got my eye on you, Sam Woollman," she said. And she kept it on him for the rest of the lesson.

After break, the class worked on individual worksheets on Tudor homes, which provided sufficient cover for Sam to get out his list. He studied it, corrected Jamie's spelling and doodled in the margin.

"We won't be able to read it soon," Jamie complained.

Leaning forward in his seat, Sam spoke to Victoria Topping on the next table.

"Hey, Topcat! Let's borrow your rubber."

"Don't you have one of your own?"

"I wouldn't be asking if I did."

"Have you borrowed it before?"

"No," said Sam.

Victoria opened a small notebook. On the front was written "My renting-out-my-rubber book."

"It'll cost you 2p."

"2p? 2p! Forget it. 2p, to borrow a rubber!"

"We're saving up," said Serafina, the girl next to her.

"To buy a horse," Victoria explained.

"Haven't you had enough of falling off horses?"

Victoria looked down her nose at Sam. "I didn't fall off, I was thrown. There is a difference, you know."

"I know all about horses," said Sam. "You seem to forget my mum's got four. Who d'you think taught you to ride?"

"Yes, well," she said, dismissing Sam, "some people might say that your mum has four horses, three children and a *donkey*."

Victoria turned back to her work. Her three friends, Zoe, Chloe and Serafina, otherwise known as the vice squad, started to giggle.

Sam searched for a suitably crushing reply, but failed to come up with one. It never paid to trade insults with Victoria Topping, she was too good at it. He leant back in his chair and pretended he wasn't in the least bit bothered.

But Luke couldn't resist waggling his hands, like a pair of ears, on top of his head. "Eeee-Aawww. Eeee-Aawww."

"Get on with your work, Luke Harman," said

the teacher, looking up from her desk. "We don't need your farmyard impressions just now, thank you very much."

"No, Hormone, we don't. Thank you very much," said Sam.

Luke ducked his head to hide the blush which was already travelling across his face. Sam and Jamie grinned at one another, licked their fingers and mimed a number one. They kept a tally of how many times a day they could make Luke blush. It often ran into double figures.

Later, when it was safe to talk again, Sam said, "OK. To business. Have you got your photos yet?"

Jamie and Luke both shook their heads.

"Anything I've got'd be a complete giveaway. I look straight out of playschool in most of mine," said Jamie.

"I hate having my photo taken," agreed Luke.

"Look, you dodos, it's important so get on to it, right."

Sam was starting to throw his weight around which always got under Jamie's skin.

"Let's see yours, then."

"It's at home," Sam mumbled, turning his attention back to the list. "OK, one and two: We've got to find someone else who's got their own instrument. Keyboard would be good, or drums."

Luke chewed his pen and tried to look thoughtful, but he hadn't a clue. The only people he knew who played instruments were in the school orchestra and scraped away at violins and things.

"What about KitKat?" said Jamie.

"Kat Harris!" said Sam, looking across the classroom at her. "That little nerd."

"She's not *that* small." She was the same height as Jamie.

"Blu-tack? Blu-tack plays the drums?" said Luke. Kat was notorious for chewing things: rubbers, balsa-wood, blotting paper, blu-tack, her own hair – everything went into her mouth. "She's weird."

"She is not. Anyway, she can play the drums. She's got a full set."

"Dream on," said Sam. "She'd have a job seeing over the top."

"Get lost." Jamie easily tired of jokes about size.

Luke felt the usual pull to ease the atmosphere between his two friends. "So, what's next?"

"Somewhere to practice," said Sam. "That's cool. I've got that in hand."

"What's number four?" asked Luke.

"Transport," said Sam.

"Money again!"

"I suppose you'll take care of that an' all," said Jamie.

"I've been thinking about it," said Sam, leaning back in his chair. "Either of you two bozos got a rubber we can rent out?"

At lunchtime Luke recounted, in minute detail, his brilliant trick on his sister that morning.

"Wick-ed," said Sam, who had sisters of his own.

"But what was the point?" asked Jamie, who hadn't.

"The point, Dumbo," said Sam, "is that sisters are the worst pain in the world. Sisters, especially younger sisters, are like a bad smell or a dreadful disease or lousy weather. You can't do a lot about them. You can't ever get rid of them. But you can have a great time making them suffer. That's what they're for, sisters – to suffer – as much and as often as possible."

When Sam finished, he and Luke skinned palms in acknowledgement of a shared enemy.

"Oh, man. That is the truth," said Luke. This

was what Luke loved about Sam, that he could put things into words, so much better than Luke could. He gave Sam an admiring punch.

Jamie shrugged. "I still don't see the point."

Sam grabbed Jamie's head and tucked it into his armpit where it just fitted. Sam peered into Jamie's ear and knocked on his head "Is there anyone in?" he called. "Anyone at home? Anyone available for comment?"

Jamie shrieked to be let go. Luke stood by, laughing.

Miss Gordon, the teacher on playground duty, walked past. "Sam Woollman, what are you doing to Jamie Jackson's head?"

"Just trying to unscrew it, Miss." Sam smiled innocently and released Jamie.

Luke helpfully straightened out Jamie's clothes and smoothed his hair. Jamie pushed him away. "Get off."

"People's heads don't unscrew, Sam," she replied, "usually."

"No," said Sam. "But it seemed worth a try."

By the end of the afternoon, Sam felt fit to burst with frustration. Mrs Carter-Coombes had kept such a close eye on him he'd been unable to skive for five minutes. Then she'd subjected them to an afternoon storytime which had him feeling like a five-year-old, sitting on a rug, sucking his thumb. For Sam, destined as he was for stardom, it had been a very humiliating experience. He couldn't wait to get away. He was out of his seat several times before the class was dismissed.

"*Someone* seems to have forgotten where his bottom is!" said Mrs Carter-Coombes. Jamie pulled Sam back into his seat and the class was finally allowed to go.

"*Someone* seems to have forgotten where his bottom is," Victoria Topping repeated at full volume as they walked down the corridor. "I can't imagine how," she added, "with a bottom that size."

Her friends dutifully burst into giggles. Sam, really mad now, elbowed Victoria and her gang roughly aside.

"Mind my broken arm, you moron!" she called after him, but Sam strode on. Luke and Jamie followed in Sam's wake. As they passed, Zoe and Chloe patted Jamie on the head. Jamie curled his lip and snarled.

"Careful," said Luke. "He bites."

The three boys overtook Kat Harris walking with her hands in her pockets and her head down as if she'd dropped something on the floor and was looking for it.

"If she's a drummer," said Sam, "I'm a monkey's uncle."

"No comment," said Jamie.

"Anyway, she's a girl," said Sam.

"So?"

"We don't want girls in our band."

Jamie shrugged, he couldn't be bothered arguing. Luke looked disappointed but said nothing. He'd have liked to have girls in the band. Well, one girl in particular, but he was keeping that information close to his chest.

"We don't want girls," Sam continued, "because girls mean trouble. T-R-O-U-B-L-E. Trouble. That's why. We're having no girls in this band. Never, not ever. Have you got that?"

"Yeah, yeah," said Jamie. "Loud and clear."

CHAPTER FIVE

After school, Sam and Luke lounged on Jamie's bed, while he sat at his computer. He could wipe out a whole army of aliens in one minute ten seconds flat, but he was trying to improve on this. He was interrupted, however, by a puzzle book winging its way across the room, hitting him on the back of the head.

"Pack it in!" he yelled.

"Well, pay attention, then. This is more important than stupid computer games." Sam waved the precious list in the air.

Jamie didn't even bother to argue. He knew from experience that anything Sam wasn't interested in was by definition "stupid". He turned and faced them. "Well, go on then. Where're we up to?"

"We still need someone else for the band. And don't suggest any girls."

"If we can't have girls, what are we gonna do about dancers?"

"Yeah," Luke agreed. "We'll have to have girls for that . . . I s'pose," he added, embarrassed by his own enthusiasm.

Now he'd given himself away.

"Who did you have in mind, Lulu?" asked Jamie, grinning.

Luke looked like an over-ripe tomato.

"Aww, look. Hormone's got the hots." Sam pushed Luke across the bed. "Who is it, then?" He twisted Luke's arm behind his back.

Luke had Chloe Fisher in mind, but he'd have died before admitting it.

"I bet it's V for Victory," said Jamie. This was just one of their names for Victoria Topping.

"Get lost," said Luke, jumping off the bed. The joke had already gone too far for his liking.

"Top Cat's too much for Lulu," said Sam.

It was true. Luke was privately terrified of her.

"Do you remember when she broke that egg on your head in cookery?" said Jamie.

"Yeah. Yeah." Luke suspected he'd never be allowed to forget it.

"I'd like to break an egg on *her* head," said Sam. "Better still, a couple down her neck."

"One on each of her 'you-know-whats'," said Luke.

"*You-know-whats!*" repeated Jamie disdainfully, which started Luke off blushing again.

"Let's do it," said Sam.

"Yeah," said Luke, beside himself with excitement.

"As if you'd dare," said Jamie. "She'd flatten you with her plaster."

"Let her try. We'd break her other arm," said Sam.

"You're all talk, you pair," said Jamie, turning his back on them. He did an imitation of a terrified Victoria. "Oh, Spam, don't hurt me. Oh, Hormone, I won't grass."

Sam and Luke smiled, silently shook hands, then descended on Jamie from behind.

"You're dead!" they shouted.

Jamie's mum put her head round the door and found the boys in a scrum on the floor, Jamie on the bottom.

"Is everyone all right in here?"

"It's OK, Mum," came Jamie's strangled cry. "It's cool."

Luke and Sam looked up, grinning.

"Don't worry, Mrs Jackson. His head doesn't come off."

"We tried earlier at school."

"Well, that's a relief," she said.

Ten minutes later the boys were walking down the road towards the shopping precinct, escorting Luke to his guitar lesson. He didn't want those two truffles hanging around Crumpet's house, making faces through the window, or ringing the doorbell in the middle of his lesson and running off, which they had been known to do, but he couldn't seem to shake them off.

"Can't this wait till tomorrow?"

"No, it can't," said Sam. "We're on a tight deadline here. I don't think you two screwballs have quite grasped how much there is to do. This tape has to be in next week and we still haven't got a band together."

Jamie and Luke mimed an outbreak of yawning.

Sam gave them a world-weary look which his dad often used on him.

43

When the boys reached the shops, Jamie headed into the newsagent's to pick up his mum's magazines.

"We could buy some tapes, while we're here," said Sam. "Got any dosh?"

"No, I haven't and I'm gonna be late," Luke grumbled.

"Don't be such a gherkin. We'll only be a minute," said Sam, following Jamie in.

Luke was starting to feel edgy. He'd hardly touched his guitar since his last lesson. He leant against the wall and started to practise his latest piece. An old lady with a dog came by and gave him twenty pence. "I don't usually approve of busking," she said, "but you look a nice boy and I can see you're trying."

Luke was amazed. Twenty pence! He glanced around sheepishly and started again. A small crowd gathered and one or two people threw coins at his feet, which embarrassed Luke, but he wasn't too embarrassed to pick them up.

When Sam and Jamie came out of the shop, Luke stopped abruptly and the crowd quickly dispersed.

"What's going on here?" Sam demanded.

"Man, you're never gonna believe this." Luke

could hardly get the words out. He showed them the 32p he had collected.

"Fantastic!" Sam took the money from Luke and gave it to Jamie. "Well, that'll help pay for the tapes."

Luke stared at his empty hand. Money always slipped through this fingers, but this was the fastest yet.

"What d'you mean? I just earned that money."

"Yeah, well, you can get down here every night after school and earn some more. I told you, didn't I, how easy it'd be?"

Luke brightened. He *would* come again, but next time he wouldn't tell this pair of ear-plugs. And he'd keep the money for himself.

At the top of the hill, the boys passed Chloe Fisher and Zoe Potter walking Zoe's dog. The two groups slowed down and circled each other.

"Can you play that guitar?" Zoe asked Luke.

"'Course he can," said Sam.

"He's just been busking outside Booth's," said Jamie.

Luke wished Jamie hadn't passed on that piece of information.

"Did you get anything?" asked Chloe.

Luke jiggled his head a bit. "Thirty-two p," he said. Both girls laughed at this, but Luke couldn't see why.

"We're starting a band, you know," said Sam.

"Hmmm." The girls were impressed.

When Luke said, "Fireballs from Hell," the girls burst out laughing.

"What's so funny?" said Sam.

"Nothing. Nothing," they assured him.

"We've entered *Smash Hits*' competition." Sam waved the pack of blank tapes. "We're making a demo tape."

Luke invited them to their first gig; Jamie promised them free tickets.

"You can start our fan club, if you like," said Sam.

The girls started to move off. Under her breath they heard Zoe say, "Is he serious?"

By now the boys were feeling quite hysterical, and burst into song. But then Luke noticed the time and began to run, his guitar banging against his thigh.

"See you, Stink Bombs!" he called.

But Sam and Jamie soon caught him up and each grabbed an arm.

"You can't get rid of us that easily, Dog Breath."

"'Fraid not, Crumb Head."

Luke resigned himself to the inevitable and all three boys arrived at Crumpet's house together. Luke was relieved when the door opened and he was able to disappear inside.

Zoe and Chloe walked to the park and let the dog off her lead. The dog quickly got down to the serious business of sniffing her way round the perimeter of the grass while the girls sat on a bench watching her.

"Sam Woollman is such a wally," said Zoe.

Chloe nodded. "Jamjar's all right."

"He's sweet."

"Luke's OK."

"Hormone! He's a div."

"He's not that bad."

"You fancy him!"

Chloe was quickly on her guard. One careless word and Victoria would find out. Then she'd never hear the end of it.

"No I do *not*," she said. "Don't be a twit."

But Zoe wasn't fooled. "You'll have to ask him if you can be in his band."

Chloe had already begun to think about that as a possibility.

"I wouldn't mind," said Zoe, striking up a pose. "I've always fancied myself in a rock band."

Chloe looked sideways at her. You could never tell when Zoe was serious.

"We could ask them," Chloe suggested, tentatively.

"Let's ask Top Cat first. Fireballs from Hell! I can't wait to tell her. Honestly, she'll die."

Chloe didn't answer. Once Victoria got hold of the news, she wouldn't be happy until she was running the show. There were often things Chloe wished they didn't have to tell Victoria, and this was one of them.

CHAPTER SIX

Sam was slumped in front of the television watching American football when his dad came in, wiping his hands clean on a bit of old rag.

"Isn't it time he was in bed?"

"You try," said Sam's mum. "He doesn't listen to me."

"He's completely out of control."

Sam's mum laughed. Sam looked as out of control as a slug.

"I am here, you know." Sam's mum and dad often talked about him as if he wasn't.

"Bed," said his dad, pointing a still oily finger.

"Aw, Dad!"

Sam's dad gave him a warning look. "Bed!" he repeated.

It was deeply insulting, Sam felt, when you were on the verge of international stardom, to be packed off to bed before ten o'clock. He had consistently tried to educate his parents on the matter. But, on this occasion, Sam decided to cooperate.

"Anything you say, Boss." He eased himself out of the chair, straightened the chair back, plumped up the cushions and offered the seat to his dad. His parents looked at one another in surprise.

"What's he after?"

"Well, since you asked, we were wondering . . ."

"Who's we?"

"Me and Luke and Jamie."

"Ah, The Three Musketeers."

". . . we were just wondering . . ."

"No," said his dad.

"You don't know what I was gonna ask."

"Whatever it was, the answer's No!"

"Oh, Geoff, give him a chance," said Sam's mum.

"Yeah, Geoff, give us a chance," said Sam.

Sam's dad gave him another warning; his mum smiled.

"We just want to borrow one of the sheds."

"Borrow a shed! What for?" His dad kept his eyes on the TV screen, determined not to commit himself.

"Our band-practice."

"Ahhh." The penny had finally dropped. "Would this be the same band that's going to make us so rich *I* can retire for life? Is it that band you're talking about?"

"You wait. We're going to be really big. Bigger than Iron Maiden, bigger than Guns 'n' Roses, bigger than Bon Jovi . . ."

"Who?" Sam's dad was unimpressed. He thought most of Sam's music sounded as if someone was digging up the road.

"You're just a dinosaur, you are."

"Yes, well, this dinosaur still rules the world, so you'd better get up those stairs, lad, before *you* become extinct."

"Aw, Dad, can we?"

"Oh, let him, Geoff. At least that way we might get him to bed."

"*If* he clears it out."

"Sure thing," said Sam.

"*And* he keeps the racket down."

"Whatever you say, Boss."

"And he gets to bed – *now!*"

"I'm as good as gone!" Sam raced out of the

room sideways, like a cartoon character.

His dad shook his head. "I am seriously worried about that boy."

Immediately Sam reappeared, skidding to a halt. "And can we have the tape-deck?"

"Get lost," said his dad.

"And the speakers? And the extension lead?"

"Why don't you ever quit while you're winning?" said his mum.

"Go on, Dad. It'll all be worth it, you'll see."

"Go to bed," said his mum and dad in unison.

Sam waved and blew kisses all the way up the stairs. "'Night fans."

"Goodnight," said his mum, closing the door on him.

Sam's dad clutched his head. "What is he like?"

His wife put a comforting arm round his shoulders. "His dad, of course. Chip off the old block, I'd say."

Sam lay in bed, hugging himself with delight. OK, his dad hadn't actually said yes to everything. But he hadn't said no, either. It was as good as settled.

Tomorrow they could clear the shed and then, as soon as they found another band member, they'd be ready to start. With a few practices they could have the tape done by next week. He was sure they'd get through. Oh, man! He couldn't wait.

"Well, Sam Woollman, what have you got to say for yourself? Are you excellent, or what!"

Sam answered with absolute conviction, "Excellent. And getting better every day."

Luke was in bed too and wide awake, wrestling with his conscience. He had five pounds in a biscuit tin on top of his wardrobe. The list of things they needed for the band seemed endless: amplifiers, microphones, transport, publicity . . .

Five pounds wouldn't go far, but it was a start. But Luke needed that money himself; he was desperate for batteries. Luke had been working on a burglar-proof box to keep his private belongings in. The idea was, whenever Public Enemy Number One tried to interfere with it, a warning bell would ring and, if he could get it right, a flashing light, too. But all his batteries were flat. He really needed new ones.

Of course, Sam and Jamie didn't have to know about the five pounds. The trouble was, Luke couldn't keep a secret to save his life. It was easy for those two. Sam could earn money cleaning out his mum's horses, if he wasn't such an idle waster. And Jamie's mum gave him anything he wanted: video games, a computer, Nike trainers. Luke could see it wasn't easy for Jamie, having no dad and that. But his mum did spoil him.

Things would be so different when they were famous. No one would be able to tell Luke what to spend his money on. He'd do *exactly* as he pleased.

Luke drifted into sleep compiling a list of all the things he'd ever wanted and never been allowed: electric guitar, air rifle, stereo system, remote-control car, leather jacket, pen-knife, mountain bike, diamond stud . . .

Jamie's mum had been in twice earlier to tell him to put out his light. But he knew she had one of her charity groups meeting in the lounge, so he was safe for a while. He turned on his computer. He still hadn't started on the publicity material he'd promised Sam. He ought to get on with it.

"Press-packs. You know the kind of thing," Sam told him. "Posters, photos, background info, interesting facts about us."

"Interesting facts? Are there any?"

"What d'you mean?" said Luke.

"About you bowls of porridge?"

"You call yourself a writer," Sam snapped. "Make some up. And I want it tomorrow."

Well, he'd do it in a minute. He'd just take another look at his novel first. Bert Lurch-Hooter had made yet another spectacular recovery. Houdini-style, he'd escaped from the crate and swum over a mile to the coast – Bert was a demon swimmer too! – where he'd dragged his exhausted body ashore.

Now Bert and his slow-witted but loyal assistant, Bonehead, were back on the trail of The Big Boss Man. They had discovered a container lorry, packed with pirate video games destined for South America, and at this moment they were hiding inside.

Jamie continued:

With one swing of his ham-like fist, Ghoul slammed the door shut and fastened the bolts. The Weasel started up the engine and Bert and Bonehead were hurled out of their hiding place.

"How will we get out of here, Chief?" asked Bonehead.

Good question, thought Jamie. He was waiting for inspiration, when he heard voices in the hall saying goodbye, followed by his mum's footsteps coming towards his room.

"Rats!" said Jamie. He pressed the Save key before diving under his quilt.

"Oh, Jamie!" His mum sighed. She tip-toed across the room, turned off the monitor and crept out.

"Take the discs out *before* you turn it off," came a strangled voice from under the covers.

"I thought *you* were asleep."

"I am."

"That's all right, then," said his mum, closing the door.

Lying in the dark, Jamie remembered he'd still not done the publicity pack. Well, what was the point, anyway? They hadn't even got a proper band together yet. Jamie seriously doubted that they ever would, with Spam in charge. Now, if *he* was running things . . .

CHAPTER SEVEN

Mrs Carter-Coombes had told Billy Brewer three times already to "Sit down!" in his place. He kept hanging around Victoria's table, desperate to write his name on her plaster cast. She was due to have it taken off soon, so she had finally agreed to let her friends autograph it. Her friends did not include Billy.

"Just go away," she said.

"Aw, go on. You're letting all this lot." Billy nodded towards the Vice Squad who were practising their signatures until they were neat enough to satisfy Victoria. "I won't do any rude jokes," he promised.

Victoria sighed and started reading.

"I'll pay you."

Victoria stopped reading. "How much?"

"Twenty pence."

"Twenty-five."

"All right. It's a deal."

"And I want the money first," she said.

"I'll bring it this afternoon."

"You won't see this afternoon if I have to tell you one more time to stay in your seat, Billy Brewer," said the teacher, descending on Billy for the fourth time that morning.

Sam watched Billy and shook his head. "Brewer'll end up with handles like Hormone's if he keeps on."

Luke winced and instinctively covered his ears.

The list was out on the table. By now it had been folded and unfolded so many times it looked faded and worn, like an ancient treasure map. Sam had enjoyed crossing off *somewhere to practise* but now even he was beginning to acknowledge that lack of money was a bit of a problem.

"If one of *us* broke an arm, or better still a leg," he suggested, "we could charge people to sign it."

"Are you volunteering?" asked Jamie.

"It's nothing, falling off a horse."

"That's all you know," said Victoria, who never missed a thing. "I *do* know because I've done it lots of times."

"Twice actually," Chloe corrected her, under her breath. Luke heard and grinned at her, then blushed at his own audacity. It made his day when Chloe smiled back.

"It's one of the hazards of horse-riding," said Victoria. "My uncle once broke his leg so badly that the bone came through the skin and stuck out through his jodhpurs."

Victoria had a collection of personal disasters that had befallen people she knew; she used them to shock her friends. The other girls groaned and pretended to be sick.

The boys rolled their eyes and turned away. But it had reminded Sam of a story of his own, where Victoria was feeding Brookside, one of his mum's horses, and it had leaned forward and tried to bite her.

"Right in the middle of her chest," laughed Sam.

"She could have lost her you-know-whats," gasped Luke.

"Victoria Topless," Jamie guffawed.

Terrified Victoria might hear, Luke put his hand over Jamie's mouth.

"Get off!" said Jamie, struggling to breathe.

"And you three can get on with your work," said the teacher.

The boys turned back to their books. When it was safe, Sam drew two circles with dots in the middle in his margin and an arrow with the letters YKWs beside it. He angled his book to show Jamie, who spluttered and tried to turn it into a cough. Mrs Carter-Coombes looked over her glasses at him. "I'm watching you," she said.

After lunch, the boys made their way to the school kitchen where, to their disgust, they found themselves in a cookery group with the dreaded Vice Squad. They were supervised by Mrs Tulliver, Terry Tulliver's mum, who came into school to help out.

Victoria and her friends, wearing aprons and with sleeves rolled up, were neatly setting out everything in front of them, as if they'd been invited to do a TV cookery demonstration.

Sam was telling the others how he'd persuaded his dad to lend them the shed and how they'd better get over to his house by six, or sooner, to help clear it out.

"What's the point?" said Jamie. "We still don't have a band yet."

"We will," said Sam, chasing a lump of margarine round his bowl. It was all over his hands and half-way up the sleeves of his jacket.

"You'd be better off with soft margarine," was Jamie's advice.

"Oh, hark at Flora Man," said Sam, flinging in his sugar and beating the mixture to death.

"It's enough to put you off food for life watching those morons cooking," said Victoria over her shoulder.

Sam lifted his spoon, which was heaped with cake mixture, and pretended to flick it at Victoria's back. He pretended so well that some of it actually connected. A huge dollop landed in Victoria's ponytail.

"Shot!" said Luke.

"You're dead," said Jamie, shaking his head in disbelief.

Victoria felt the hit, turned round and stepped into the mixture as some of it landed on the floor.

"You idiot! You absolute imbecile. You half-wit, you lame-brain . . ."

"Victoria!" said Mrs Tulliver, shocked.

"It's him. Look what he did to me."

"Oh, Sam."

"It was an accident."

"Well, let's get you cleaned up," said Mrs Tulliver, trying to restore order. These cookery lessons were always a race against the clock. The cakes should have been in the oven minutes ago. But Victoria wasn't that easily satisfied. "Isn't he going to apologize?"

"Yes. Come along, Sam, just apologize and then we can get on."

Everyone in the kitchen turned to watch them. It was like a shoot-out at the OK Corral. Sam considered refusing, but couldn't see how he might get away with it. He puffed out his cheeks, then reluctantly mumbled, "Sorry."

"Good," said Mrs Tulliver briskly. "Now, everyone get a move on. Chop, chop."

Jamie and Luke watched Sam out of the corners of their eyes. They could tell how mad he was by the way he gripped the wooden spoon.

"Ignore her," said Luke, giving him a friendly punch.

"She's not worth the bother," Jamie agreeed.

"None of them are," snarled Sam. "I hate *girls*." He beat the cake mixture until it was in danger of curdling.

Luke sighed. Where once he would have laughed at Sam and agreed with him, he now felt nothing but irritation. Sam was getting to be a bit boring on the subject and Luke was coming close to telling him so.

Once their cakes were in the oven, Sam and Luke sat on the worktop resting. They sent Jamie to do their washing-up.

"Why me?" he asked, loaded up with bowls and spoons.

"Because you're the smallest," said Sam.

They watched Jamie across the kitchen, chatting away like best mates with the Vice Squad. He was up to his elbows in soap-suds while the girls stood round, drying his dishes for him.

"Look at him," said Sam. "He's more like a girl than a girl."

"He's all right," said Luke, loyally.

When Jamie came back, Sam demanded to know what they'd been talking about.

"I asked them if they wanted to be dancers for The Band."

"You did *what*!"

"They're thinking about it. They haven't decided yet."

"You asked Victoria Topping?" said Luke incredulously.

"No, of course not. The others."

Sam looked set to explode. "You're fired!"

"What?"

"Fired, from the band."

"Suits me," said Jamie.

"Aw, come on," said Luke, trying to make peace.

"He's fired."

"I heard you the first time. Although I don't see how you can be fired from something that doesn't exist."

"Look, he's only asked them. We don't have to have them."

"We're not having them."

"So who do you suggest?" asked Jamie. "At least this lot can dance, they all go to dance club. And they can sing, they're all in the choir. And none of them looks like the back of a bus."

"He's got a point," said Luke.

"And we agreed we'd need girls as dancers."

"We did."

"*And* we're short of time," Jamie reminded Sam.

"He's right," said Luke.

"He's *fired*," said Sam.

★　　★　　★

As Sam and Luke crossed the playground, they saw Jamie ahead of them walking home with Kat Harris.

"Look at that pair of gnomes," said Sam.

"Oh, give it a rest," said Luke.

"If she's a drummer, I'll eat my boxer-shorts."

"That'll be worth seeing."

"As for him . . ."

"Just give him a chance," said Luke. He was sick of being caught in the middle.

"He's had his chance and he's blown it. He's finished, dead meat, old news, understand? From now on it's just the two of us."

Luke looked at him in disbelief. "Dream on."

"Of course, you'll have to do something about your image. Dye your hair, get a nose-ring. Get a tattoo. MADE IN BRITAIN – on your bum! Then you can do moonies."

Luke watched Sam, doubled up, laughing at his own joke.

"And that's just where you can put your band," he told him.

Luke walked off. He'd had more than enough of Sam for one day.

CHAPTER EIGHT

"It's come. It's come!" Sam shouted, waving the form in the air. He raced down the stairs two at a time. His little sisters lay across the landing in a pair of sleeping bags, sucking their thumbs, playing at being asleep.

"Mum! Mum!" they squealed. "Sam trod on our hair."

"What am I supposed to do? If you will lie in the way?"

Sam's mum tried to make herself heard over the din. "What on earth's going on?"

Sam followed her voice into the kitchen. "The form from *Smash Hits*, it's come." He waved it under her nose.

"Oh, that's nice." She was rather distracted because she was changing Ruby's nappy. Sam turned away in disgust.

"Nice! Nice? Is that all you can say?" Sam wanted someone to share his excitement. He wanted to share it with Luke, but he couldn't now they'd fallen out.

"What is it?" asked his sisters, running in, but Sam withered them with a glance.

"Nothing to do with kids," he snarled and walked into the lounge. They were so stupid, he thought, and as they got older they'd get worse, like the Vice Squad. Other poor boys, like him and Luke, would end up at each other's throats all because of those two specimens.

Girls were the cause of most of life's troubles, it seemed to Sam. If Jacko hadn't invited them into the band, Sam wouldn't be sitting here now feeling he couldn't ring up and share this exciting news with his friends.

Sam went back upstairs to lie on his bed. He picked up his microphone.

"Can you tell us about the early days, before you were so famous?" asked the interviewer.

Sam began to relax. "My dad had this old shed. Me and the boys used to hang out there, playing a few riffs, improvising a few numbers.

Those were ace times." Sam smiled fondly to himself.

"*Sounds great*," said the interviewer.

"Yeah, well it was, *most* of the time, until *girls* got involved."

Sam's sisters walked past his bedroom door, carrying plates and beakers with curly straws in them, wearing bathing costumes and riding hats and their mum's high heels.

What a pair of clowns, Sam thought.

"Great cakes, Spam," said Kirsty.

"Deee-licious," said Keira.

"Go and get me one."

"All gone," said Kirsty, licking her fingers.

"What!" Sam jumped up and raced downstairs. The empty box sat on the kitchen table. "They ate my cakes! They ate all my cakes!" The frustrations of the day finally came to the boil. "That's it! That is *it*!" Sam charged out of the house.

"Where are you going?" his mum shouted after him.

"*Out!*" yelled Sam, slamming the door behind him.

Luke was in his bedroom, wiring up his burglar alarm. He'd got the light to flash and now he had the buzzer working, but so far he hadn't managed both together. Luke had felt no conscience about going out to buy his battery when he got in from school. Why should *he* hang on to his money when Sam was being such a bozo? He tightened a connection and suddenly a steady buzzing coincided with a flashing light. "Bullseye!" He heard a heavy tread running up the stairs, and his name being called.

"Luke, you there?"

Luke cursed and scrambled to hide his circuit but Sam was inside the room before he had the chance.

"Haven't you ever heard of knocking?"

Clearly Luke was still in a razz. "Come on, Hormone, chill out. What're you up to?"

"Nothing," said Luke, bundling his bits together.

"Show us."

"It's nothing. It's just a burglar alarm to keep Public Enemy Number One out of my private things."

"What private things?" Sam didn't know Luke had any private things. If he had, he'd been holding out on him.

Luke refused to be drawn. He pushed the box under his bed and got up. "Anyway, what do you want?"

Sam showed Luke the application form.

Luke pretended he wasn't in the least bit interested.

"Come on. You're not going to keep this up, are you?"

Luke shrugged. "Jamie's right. What's the point? You haven't got a band together yet and at this rate you never will."

"There's you and me."

Luke gave him a look and folded his arms.

"OK. OK. *And* Jacko."

"What about Kat Harris?"

Sam hesitated, his shoulders drooped, but he saw Luke's determined expression.

"OK," he said. "It's cool by me."

"Good," said Luke. "It's about time you came to your senses. Let's go, then."

Once they'd collected Jamie, the three boys walked along, hands in their pockets, heads bent.

Sam was forced to shorten his stride because Luke was determined they wouldn't leave Jamie behind.

"Where are we going now?" asked Sam.

Luke shrugged. He was just walking.

"For KitKat," said Jamie.

"What, now?" Sam would have liked a bit more time to get his head round this. "I don't go calling for girls. You can go if you like, but leave me out."

You'd have thought Jamie had suggested they visit Dracula's mother. Even Luke seemed uneasy. "She might be having her tea."

"Don't worry. She won't eat *you*. She's a vegetarian."

Kat's mum opened the door. "Hello, Jamie," she said and with a wave of her arm directed the boys upstairs. "Just follow the yellow brick road . . ."

Luke and Sam smirked at each other and followed Jamie up a dull gold-coloured carpet which wound its way for three flights up to the attic.

The Harrises lived in a four-storey terraced house and the boys felt as if they'd climbed Everest by the time they came to Kat's room, which was in the roof. As they reached the door they could hear a dull thudding. When Jamie opened the door the noise almost deafened them. He started to grin. Sam knew what he was thinking; it was written all over his face: I told you.

Luke whispered in Sam's ear, "Prepare to eat your boxer-shorts."

★   ★   ★

Kat was sitting at a full-size drum kit which, as Sam predicted, she could only just reach, let alone see over the top of. But she was beating the drums with a wild energy that immediately made the boys think of Animal out of the Muppets. She was wearing a baseball cap and a huge pair of glasses, with no glass in them. She looked completely crazy. Bogus, totally weird, thought Sam.

"Outrageous," said Luke.

Both boys watched, open-mouthed.

As soon as she spotted them, Kat stopped dead. Jamie and Kat nodded to each other, Luke and Sam unashamedly stared round the room. The walls were plastered with posters of pop groups and the room itself, even by their standards, was an absolute tip. When they'd finished staring they both dropped their eyes to the carpet and an awkward silence followed.

Jamie rushed in to fill it. "D'you want to join our band?"

There was a fierce intake of breath from Sam. "I'll do the asking. This is my band, in case you've forgotten."

Jamie just shrugged. Luke grinned encouragingly at Kat. She threw back her head, sucked in her cheeks and looked at the ceiling for what seemed like ages.

"Who's in it?" she finally asked.

"Just us three," said Sam.

"What's it called?"

Sam began to huff and puff. It was like *Twenty Questions*.

"Fireballs from Hell," said Jamie, cringing in mock embarrassment.

"Not much of a name," said Kat. Sam raised his eyes to the roof. She didn't believe in beating about the bush.

"We might change it," said Luke.

"We will not," said Sam.

"We're going in for a competition," said Jamie.

"And we're going to *win* it," Sam added.

"It's in *Smash Hits*," said Luke. "You know, the magazine."

"I know," said Kat.

"So?" The boys waited for a verdict.

"OK. Count me in."

"Yeah!" All three boys skinned palms. Sam took out his list and drew a thick line through numbers one and two – *more instruments and people to play them.*

"Be at my place, tonight at six," Sam told Kat. "We've got to clear the shed so we can practise."

"We've got to make a demo tape," Luke added proudly.

"And a video," said Sam.

"A video?"

"'Course. It's cool. I've got the technology. Don't worry."

Jamie shook his head and tried not to laugh. "What planet is he on?" he whispered to Luke.

Luke smiled too. "Come on," he said, leading Sam away. "I'm going to be late for my tea. And you've got a pair of boxer-shorts for yours."

CHAPTER NINE

Luke, Jamie and Kat arrived at Sam's to find him sitting in the shed, amongst years of accumulated rubbish, strumming his guitar and singing something barely recognizable as a tune.

"You're in the wrong key," said Luke.

Sam was tempted to argue, but changed key instead.

Jamie looked round the shed. "Is this it?"

"What did you expect?"

"It's full of junk."

"Yes, well, we're going to clear it out, aren't we?"

"Where're we going to put everything?" asked Luke.

"Most of it can go to the tip. Some of it can go on a bonfire."

"I'll be in charge of that," Jamie volunteered. He loved fires; he was in his element on Bonfire Night.

"Well, let's get going then," said Luke.

"Keep your hair on," said Sam. "We've got to have a plan."

"We hardly need a plan for shifting rubbish," said Jamie, rifling through a box full of old *Car* magazines.

Kat was more interested in getting answers to some questions. "What about this band, then?"

Sam turned to her. "What about it?"

"Well, what kind of band's it gonna be? *Fireballs From Hell* sounds like a heavy metal band."

"So?" said Sam.

"I thought it was going to be a rock band."

Luke looked down and gave his usual *don't ask me* shrug.

"Yeah, well, we haven't finally decided yet," said Sam, evasively.

"Well, it's time you did," said Jamie.

"You can't really make a tape until you do," Kat pointed out.

Sam's blood began to boil. She'd only just joined and they were already ganging up on him.

"I'll decide, don't you worry. You leave it to me. You leave everything to me. It's all in hand." Sam patted the portable cassette player at his side. "Now, quit loafing around and let's see some action. Let's get this show on the road." Sam cracked an imaginary whip. Jamie and Luke rolled their eyes. With Kat there, Sam was clearly going to be even more embarrassing than usual.

With Bon Jovi belting out of Sam's cassette player, they carried out old tyres, dozens of almost-empty paint tins, a broken lawn mower, a couple of three-wheeler bikes, endless unidentifiable pieces of motor cars and loads of cardboard boxes and bits of wood. The pile filled the drive and grass alongside.

Sam and Luke, struggling with a tall pair of step-ladders, caught a spade resting across the rafters. It landed within an inch of Jamie's foot.

"Look out, you idiots!" shouted Jamie. "Are you trying to kill me? You could have had my foot off. I could have lost all my toes. I could have been maimed for life."

"Chill out," said Luke, laughing. "It missed you, didn't it?"

Jamie had a reputation for being accident-prone. Fooling around with this pair, he'd fallen in the canal and nearly drowned, broken his nose ice-skating, fallen off a swing and cut his head open and once, at school, nearly choked on a crisp because Luke made him laugh. Now they'd almost crippled him. He took off his trainer just to check.

"I'm sick of this. It's too much like hard work."

"Well, you'd better get used to it," said Sam. "This is the kind of thing roadies have to do."

"I don't wanna be a roadie. It's stupid. I want a proper job."

"You're supposed to be doing publicity," Sam reminded him.

"Yeah. Yeah. But I could do more of the organizing as well."

"What d'you mean?"

"I could fill the form in and send it off."

"It's done." Sam pointed to it on the work-bench.

Jamie picked it up. "Could I just make a suggestion?"

Sam stopped midway to the door.

"Where it says Name of Band – this is only a suggestion – but what about: Bert Lurch and the Boneheads?"

"Are you kidding?" said Luke.

"*You're* a bonehead," was Sam's verdict.

Kat started to laugh but swallowed it.

"It was only a suggestion. *Fireballs From Hell* sounds stupid."

"I don't remember asking for your opinion," said Sam. "Roadies are not paid to think. They're paid to lift and shift, so do it."

"This roadie isn't paid anything," grumbled Jamie, putting his trainer back on.

"Phew! About time," said Luke, holding his nose.

When the shed was empty, Luke picked up a brush and started sweeping it out. Jamie was outside building a bonfire. Sam was miming to the music on his tape. His fingers flew up and down the neck of his guitar. He looked up to find Kat staring at him. She was beginning to feel suspicious.

"You can *play* that guitar, can't you?"

"'Course I can. What d'you take me for?"

"Just checking," she said and went to join Jamie outside.

Sam raised his eyebrows and pulled a duckface at Luke. "You can *play* that guitar, can't you?" he repeated in a high, squeaky voice.

Luke wasn't that amused but he laughed to keep Sam happy.

Suddenly they could hear Sam's dad's voice yelling outside, and immediately identified the smell that had been drifting into the shed for some minutes. They raced outside. Flames licked up into the air and pieces of burning paper floated across the sky.

"Are you trying to burn the place down?" Sam's dad demanded.

Jamie was staring at his feet, trying to look innocent. He looked about five years old.

The fire soon died down; it had been made up almost entirely of paper, but to teach them a lesson, Sam's dad made them carry buckets of water all the way from the house, half way across the paddock to the shed.

"You're a gang of vandals. Nothing between the ears," he told them. The boys smirked at each other. Yet another of Jamie's close shaves.

Kat and Jamie headed off soon after that, but Luke decided to stick around. He and Sam sat on the workbench in the shed talking. It was quiet and a bit spooky, now it was getting dark.

"What're you thinking about?" Luke asked Sam.

"About Kat Harris being in our band."

Luke shrugged. He could live with it.

But Sam wasn't sure. "I dunno. Girls always cause trouble. It's all right if they want to call *us* names and pick fights, but if we fight back it's, "'You can't hit me, I'm a girl.'" Sam protected his chest and fluttered his eyelashes like a pair of windscreen washers on full speed. "It's all right when Jody Poole goes round the playground, kicking people in the noonahs . . ." Luke instinctively covered his, ". . . but let us touch any of them in *their* painful parts and we soon cop it," said Sam. "And they're so bossy. They always have to be in charge."

Luke looked sideways at Sam. As far as he could see this didn't only apply to girls. But Luke was barely listening to Sam. He was thinking about one girl in particular. Even though Chloe Fisher went around with the dreaded Vice Squad, she wasn't bossy. Luke couldn't imagine her kicking anyone in the noonahs.

Luke really wanted Chloe in the band, but he wouldn't admit that to Sam; he'd never hear the end of it. There were some things he couldn't share with Sam, even though they were best mates – and he didn't like that feeling.

"Let's wait and see. Give Blu-tack a chance," Luke suggested. "Sort of sale or return."

"I s'pose. But *any* bother and she's out on her B-U-M."

Luke grinned and put out his hand; Sam skinned it.

"OK. I'm off," Luke said, jumping down.

"I wondered what the smell was."

"Oh, remind me to laugh. See you tomorrow."

"Not if I smell you coming."

Luke really had to go, he was already late, but he didn't like to leave Sam looking so fed up. "Walk up the drive with us," he said.

Luke left Sam at the gate and walked on down the road, then stopped and looked back. It felt really important to make Sam laugh. He waved.

"See you, Wobble Bottom."

"See you, Pimple Brain," Sam replied.

"See you, Wee Willy."

"See you, Little Dick." Sam grinned and waved as well, imitating a passing police car, "Noo-nah! Noo-nah! Noo-nah!"

Feeling reassured, Luke set off home at a jog.

*　　*　　*

Sam walked back down his drive. He breathed in the sharp night air. To tell the truth, he wasn't fed up. He was feeling pretty pleased with the way things were going. He was really getting this band on the road.

"It must have taken some determination to get where you are now," the interviewer cut in.

"And a lot of hard work," Sam agreed.

"Well, you're obviously a pretty smooth operator." Sam grinned. *"Stunningly handsome . . ."* Sam nodded, he couldn't argue with that. *". . . and incredibly talented. Where do you think you got it all from?"*

A voice rose out of the dark, "Your father probably." Sam's dad walked out of the shadows, and matching his step to Sam's, gripped him by the arm and frog-marched him towards the house. "What sort of time do you call this to come in?"

"Late?" suggested Sam.

"Pumpkin time. Bed! Now! Before you turn into one."

Sam didn't argue. He needed to keep his dad sweet. He still wanted to borrow the camcorder. He walked straight through the house and up the stairs.

"Goodnight, Mum," he said on his way.

"Where's *he* been?"

"How do I know?" said his dad. "The boy's a mystery to me. Always has been and probably always will be."

CHAPTER TEN

It was lunchtime, a couple of days later, and the boys were sitting on the mound on the school field. Close by, a fight was going on between two gangs of five-year-olds, and two nervous dinner ladies were valiantly trying to put a stop to it.

"OK, let's have a look at these photos," said Sam. The other two reluctantly handed them over.

"Is this the best you can do? These are pathetic. Hormone looks like Little Lord Fauntleroy and you look like Kermit the Frog."

"Yours is no better," said Jamie. "You look like a prize prat."

"At least I don't look straight out of play-school."

There was no answer to that. Luke and Jamie couldn't help looking young for their age.

Sam groaned. "Oh, forget it. I'll do something with them." Luke had visions of Sam adding a couple of moustaches and an eyepatch. "Tell Kat to bring hers when she comes with her drums tonight."

"Tell her yourself." Jamie was sick of Sam bossing him about.

Just then the vice squad came towards them.

Sam pulled a face. "What do these dodos want?"

But the girls ignored Sam and spoke to Jamie. "We've decided. We do want to be in your band, but on one condition."

"*My* band," Sam interrupted them. He tapped himself on the chest for emphasis. "This is my band." The girls turned to face him.

"So? What's the condition?"

"Victoria wants to be in as well."

Sam's reaction was swift and decisive. "No way. Not a chance. Over my dead body. Forget it. Don't even ask."

"Suit yourself," said Zoe. "But that's the offer.

All of us – or none of us." The girls walked away swinging their ponytails to show the boys *they* weren't bothered one way or the other.

"Well? Don't just sit there like a pair of bookends," said Sam.

Luke and Jamie said nothing, but looked mutinous.

"Oh! You'd like that bossy-boots to come in and take over our band, would you?"

"No, of course, we don't want *her*," said Jamie. "But if that's the only way we get the others, can't we just ignore her?"

"Ignore Victoria Topping and she'd walk all over your face."

"Oh, chill out you pair," said Luke. "There's no point arguing."

"I agree. Let's vote. Against?" Sam raised his own hand.

Luke hesitated, then raised his.

"Two, one. That's decided."

"Let's see what Kat thinks," said Jamie, going off to find her.

"Oh, fantastic," said Sam, throwing his hands up in the air. "Now look what you've started."

"Me?"

"Whose idea was it to include Amoeba Brain and his girlfriend? Was it mine by any chance?

No, it was yours, nobody else's, just yours. And now look where it's got us."

"Oh, wind your neck in," said Luke. He was bored with the whole subject. "Anyway, it's singing next."

Their singing teacher was Mrs Morley. She taught them great songs and today they were singing one of their favourites: The Hand Jive. Sam was really getting into it, doing all the actions.

Luke nudged Jamie and raised his eyebrows to the ceiling. Jamie covered his face in embarrassment. But Sam didn't care.

"Come on. This is good practice," he told them.

"For what?" said Jamie.

"Making idiots of ourselves," said Luke.

"You pair don't need any practice," Jamie told him. "You're already experts."

"OK, good start," Mrs Morley complimented the class. "I can see you're in the mood. Let's try some people out at the front. Now . . . who shall we put in the hot-spot today?"

She looked around the class and her eyes grew bigger and seemed about to pop out. The class was always mesmerized by Mrs Morley's eyes. Sam shot his arm up in the air and dragged Luke's up too. Luke began to glow uncomfortably, but Mrs Morley passed over them quickly. "Not this week, Sam, let's give the girls a try."

To Sam's fury, the teacher chose the Vice Squad. Victoria led her group out and they lined up, oozing confidence, and with good cause. Not only could the girls sing well, but they danced too, doing all the actions Mrs Morley had taught them with such confidence that it looked as if they'd been practising together for weeks, which in fact they had.

Sam could see the girls were just what the band needed – Victoria, even with one arm in plaster, looked professional – but he couldn't bear to admit it. He scowled and tried to find fault. He turned to his friends hoping to share some joke, but they were watching avidly, their mouths open wide in admiration.

"Oh, button up," he said. "You look as if you're catching flies."

At the end of the lesson Sam went for a walk round school to cool his temper, but when he got back to the classroom he found Kat Harris sitting in the spare place at their table.

"What's she doing here?"

The others ignored him.

"Sam Woollman, where have you been?" said the teacher. "Sit down and get on with some work. I'm sick of telling you."

Sam dragged out his chair and sat on it. Luke and Jamie exchanged glances. "Well?" Sam challenged them.

Luke, feeling cowardly, looked away, so Jamie spoke. "I think we should give Victoria and the others a go. Hormone and KitKat agree."

"Oh, they do, do they?"

Luke shifted in his chair, avoiding Sam's eye. Kat shrugged, she couldn't see what all the fuss was about.

"You saw them. They're good," said Jamie.

Sam's face set like cement. "Look," he said, banging the table for emphasis. "This band was *my* idea. *I* thought of the name. *You* didn't even want to be in it. So *I'll* decide, OK?" As his fist came down for the final time Sam found it restrained in the teacher's claw-like grip.

"I have told you, Sam Woollman, more times than enough to *get on with your work*."

Sam sighed heavily and hung his shoulders as the teacher picked up his book and gasped at the evident lack of work.

"What have you been *doing* all day?"

Sam shrugged and shook his head as if he was as puzzled as she was. Mrs Carter-Coombes handed him back his book.

"My dog could do better work than that." This was a favourite remark; they'd all heard of this talented dog before. "Office! Now!" she said, pointing.

Sam sloped off and took up an all-too-familiar position outside the Headteacher's door. He caught a glimpse of Victoria Topping gloating before Mr Burton came bustling out.

"Not you again, Sam. What is it this time?"

Under the teacher's continued gaze, Luke and Jamie got on with their maths project, which was based on data from *The Guinness Book of Records*. They pored over pictures of the heaviest man in the world and the man with the longest finger-nails.

"I wonder how he picks his nose?" said Jamie.

"That's gross," said Chloe Fisher, coming to sit on the corner of Luke's desk. He kept finding more things to show her, trying to keep her there as long as possible. Unfortunately, Sam came back and spoilt Luke's fun. He elbowed Chloe out of the way to get to his place.

"You could say excuse me," she said, going off in a huff.

"*Excuse me*," Sam repeated in a silly voice.

Luke had noticed before how Sam always had to rubbish anything if he was left out of it. But this time he wasn't prepared to let him get away with it.

"You're not as funny as you think you are, you know."

Sam glanced at Luke in surprise, but Luke turned away angrily.

"What happened?" asked Jamie, nodding towards the Head's room.

Sam gave him a pitying look. "Nothing," he said. Seeing Kat's disbelieving expression, he added, "And you can shut up."

There was an unpleasant atmosphere around the table and for the rest of the lesson they all worked in silence, an almost unheard-of event.

At home-time, Sam was still trying to make up the work he'd missed. He hardly had time to look up. "I'll see you lot tonight. Be round at my place by six, OK?"

Luke shrugged. "I'll see."

"What about the others?" Jamie asked. The

girls were still hanging around the classroom admiring Victoria's plaster.

"Forget them. They're a waste of space."

"You're a waste of space," said Luke, snatching up his bag. "Most of the time you talk complete garbage."

"I've been saying that for years," Jamie agreed.

The two boys headed off, leaving Sam open-mouthed.

"What was all that about?" He turned to Kat, who was packing up her things. "What's got into him?"

"You've upset his girlfriend."

"Girlfriend?"

Kat nodded. "Don't you notice anything?"

Sam just frowned, he was too shocked to speak.

"See you tonight," she said, zipping her jacket all the way to her chin.

Hormone? Into girls? Sam thought. That is serious. Mega-serious.

CHAPTER ELEVEN

Sam lay in a deep bath, full of his mum's Raspberry and Mango foam bath, thinking about Luke. Luke had been acting oddly of late. If Kat was right, it would explain everything. Sam reminded himself this was nothing he couldn't handle.

"Every band has its teething troubles," he told the interviewer, nonchalantly. *"You just need a strong leader to hold it all together. Fortunately for Fireballs, they've got me."*

"Are you nearly finished in that bath?" Sam heard his mum call.

"Nearly," he called back, adjusting the water supply.

Sam had devised a technique whereby, if he pushed a flannel into the plughole and left the hot tap running at just the right rate, he could keep the water warm for hours without the bath overflowing. He lay back, closed his eyes and contemplated his starry future: the satellite TV, the mobile phone, the Harley-Davidson, the private jet, the docklands flat, the castle . . .

But Sam's dreams were suddenly shattered by infant screams.

"Mum! Mum!" his sisters yelled. "Come quick. There's a river running down the stairs. And it's pink."

Luke stormed into the kitchen, throwing his bag on the floor.

"You've come home in a good mood," said his mum.

"What's for tea?"

"Chicken casserole."

"Puke."

"What's wrong with you? Have you been falling out with someone?"

"I bet it's that Fat Spam," said Lucy. Luke silenced her with an evil look, but it was too late. She'd already set their mum off.

"I don't know why you can't find some nice friends."

"Nice?"

"Other boys like you."

Luke doubted that there were any other boys like him, plagued with great sticking-out ears, embarrassing blushing fits, hopeless crushes on girls, a desperate lack of money, not to mention a disgusting sister and a nagging mum.

"I suppose it's all about that band again?"

"Him in a band!" Lucy collapsed on the table, raucously laughing. Luke gave her another blast of hate rays.

"It's like your dad says, what kind of band is it going to be if none of you ever practises?"

Oh, here we go, thought Luke. Why was it that parents never seemed happy unless they'd got you doing lessons from the moment you woke up to the moment you went to bed.

"He practises posing," said Lucy. "I've seen him."

She did a good imitation of Luke posing which made him blush and didn't improve his temper. If he stayed around his sister one more minute he was in danger of detaching her head and putting it in the chicken casserole.

"Can't we get her a muzzle fitted?" Luke asked.

His mum raised her eyebrow to warn Luke he'd gone too far.

"OK, OK, I'm going," he said.

Luke went to lie on his bed. He took out his diary and tried to think of something good to write in it. Then he remembered.

Chloe Fisher sat on my desk for ten minutes.

The moment the words were on the page he was terrified someone might see them. He scribbled them out until he'd almost made a hole in the page. Far safer to keep it all in his head; no one could read it there. Luke closed his eyes and thought about Chloe instead. A huge smile spread across his face. Suddenly the least welcome face in the world appeared round his door.

"What're you grinning about?" it asked.

"Just thinking. No law against it, is there?"

"About your girlfriend?" Lucy guessed.

Luke sat up and stared at her. How did she know? It was like living with the thought police.

"Ahhh haaa. Luke's got a girlfriend. I'm going to te-ll . . ."

Provoked beyond endurance, Luke threw his diary and caught his sister on the side of her head. She wailed like a siren.

"Mu-u-u-m!"

★   ★   ★

Jamie sat at his computer working on his story.

The container lorry came to a stop in the dockyard. Bert felt around in the dark until he found the huge, soft shape of Bonehead.

"Wake up," he whispered. "We've got to get out of here quick."

Too late, the huge doors swung open and Bert and Bonehead were blinded by daylight.

"Now, look who we've got here," said the Weasel, in his weaselly voice. For a moment Ghoul went even whiter than usual. The last time they'd seen Bert he was in a crate heading for the bottom of the sea.

"How did he escape?" he gasped.

"Never mind that," whined the Weasel. "There'll be no escaping this time. We're shipping them to South America. Three weeks in transit, nothing to eat and drink and it's Goodbye, Mr Hooter."

"Come and get your tea," Jamie heard his mum call.

"In a minute."

"Now! Come on, I've got a meeting tonight."

"Rats," cursed Jamie, dragging himself into the kitchen.

His mum was eating a salad. Jamie's sandwiches, white and crustless, sat ready on his plate. He curled back the edges to check the contents before he ate.

"I'm going to Sam's tonight," he told his mum. "The band's having its first practice."

"You're in a band? But you can't play anything."

Jamie couldn't tell his mum he was a roadie. She'd immediately assume he was going to hurt himself.

"I'm the manager," he said. "Sort of."

"Manager?" His mum was impressed.

"Well, they need somebody in charge. Luke and Sam couldn't find their way out of a paper bag on their own."

"So what do Luke and Sam play?"

"Guitars, sort of. And Kat's on drums."

"What are you calling this band?"

Jamie hesitated again. "We haven't really decided yet. Sam's got this daft idea, *Fireballs from Hell*, but what do you think of this?" He handed her a card he'd worked out on his computer.

She read aloud, "*Ghoul and the Weasels?* Honestly or *not* honestly?" Jamie rolled his eyes in despair. "Terrible," she said. "I'd stick to Fireballs."

Jamie and Luke were on their way to Sam's. They were discussing what to do about him.

"He's so stubborn. He's going to spoil everything," said Jamie. "I think you should tell him."

"Tell him what?"

"Not to be so . . . so prejudiced."

"Why me?"

"You're his best mate. He won't listen to me or Kat. He might listen to you."

Luke took a sideways glance at Jamie. He seemed to be on the level. "I dunno, I'll think about it. But maybe he's right."

"Oh, for goodness sake," said Jamie. "Don't you ever get a sore bum?"

"What with?" asked Luke, shocked.

"Sitting on the fence."

"I said I'll think about it."

"Don't strain yourself," said Jamie.

The two boys walked to Sam's barely speaking.

When they got there, there was no sign of Sam. Kat's mum and her sister Susie were just delivering her drums. The boys set to and helped Kat to carry them across to the shed. When the car was empty and the boot closed, Kat walked away with the boys.

Her mum called after her, "Have you got everything, Katie? Do you need any help?"

Kat didn't even turn round. "No, thanks."

"Can I come and watch?" called her sister, Susie.

"No! Go home." Her family always managed to embarrass her.

"Have a good evening, darling," Kat's mum called after her.

"Just go," Kat prayed under her breath.

Inside the shed, Luke and Jamie were bursting to laugh but one look at Kat's face silenced them. "Don't start," she warned. "Just don't start."

For once, the boys did as they were told. They sat and watched enviously as she assembled her drum kit. When she started to play, and the sound filled the shed and reverberated round their heads, both boys felt a surge of excitement. For the first time it all suddenly began to feel real.

CHAPTER TWELVE

Sam walked into the shed, carrying his guitar and his portable cassette player.

"Where've you been?" Jamie demanded. "We've been here hours."

Sam wasn't about to tell them that the reason he was late was that he'd been doing a bit of mopping up. As he came closer, Luke snorted and covered his nose. "Phew!"

"Get the gas masks." Jamie waved his hands in the air as if someone had just made a bad smell. Kat giggled behind her hand.

"Calm down, you pair of conkers, I've only had a bath." OK, so he'd used a squirt of his dad's 'Pour Hommes', which was a bit of a mistake after the foam bath, but he couldn't see what all the fuss was about.

"What *do* you look like?" said Jamie.

Sam was dressed in a black sweatshirt, black jeans, black baseball boots, black gloves and black sunglasses.

"This is the gear," he told them.

"Oh, funk-y," said Jamie.

"What happened to the T-shirt?" asked Luke.

"Jacko can wear that. But the band's wearing black."

"Black?" said Luke.

"Yeah, it's the image. Dead cool. Full of mystery."

Luke started to snigger.

"Full of garbage," said Jamie. "And so are you. You'll look like bank robbers."

"That's cool," said Sam.

"I dunno," said Luke. "I've got this new sweatshirt. Really ace."

Bored already, Kat yawned. She just wished they'd get round to playing something. These boys did nothing but talk.

"Are we going to get started soon? Or are you two going to spend the whole evening sorting out your wardrobes?"

The boys all turned on her in surprise.

"Just chill out," said Sam. She was getting too lippy for his liking. "We'll get started, don't you worry . . . when we've had a technical run-through. Just gotta check the equipment first."

"What a dork," said Jamie.

Sam ignored him and made a bit of a business of setting up the cassette recorder, playing a few chords, turning it off, rewinding, playing it back and adjusting the volume.

"Why don't you see if you can play anything, before you get hooked up with the technology?" said Jamie.

"OK. OK." Sam turned to Kat. "What can you play?"

"What can *you* play?"

"Anything. You choose," he told Luke.

But every time Luke made a suggestion Sam rubbished it.

"We're not playing that garbage."

Kat was getting more and more impatient.

"Just play something," Jamie told them. "Anything."

"All right!" said Sam. "*Back to Back*. Ready? One, two, three . . ."

They worked their way through the first few bars, Kat slowing down her drumming to keep pace with the boys. But the pace slowed further and further, until the playing completely petered out.

Luke tried not to laugh.

"Man, that was terrible," said Jamie. "That was worse than terrible."

"Oh, encourage us, why don't you?"

"Let's try something else," suggested Luke. "*Bat Out of Hell*."

This started rather more promisingly, but in no time the boys seemed to be playing completely different tunes.

"Hang on. Hang on. You've gone wrong," said Sam.

"*You've* gone wrong, you mean."

"You've both gone wrong," said Kat.

"For goodness sake," said Jamie. "Shut up and stop arguing."

"Who are you telling to shut up? Don't forget I'm in charge of this band."

"How could we forget? You never stop reminding us."

"Just leave this to me, will you? Now come on, let's try again."

For the next hour they persevered, playing one tune over and over again. Finally they had a run-through in which they all started together *and* finished in the same place, despite having taken different routes to get there. Jamie was nearly asleep from boredom.

"Well, what d'you think?" Sam asked him. "You could at least stay awake. You're supposed to be the flipping audience."

Jamie groaned. "Honestly? Or not honestly?"

"Thanks for nothing! We're getting there, that's the main thing. We'll have another go tomorrow."

"You expect me to sit through all this again tomorrow?" Jamie was beginning to wonder if you could actually die from boredom.

"Oh, stop wingeing," said Sam. "When we start taping, you can be in charge of that, *if* you can stay awake."

Just then Sam's dad came in, pointing to his watch. "Haven't you got any homes to go to?"

He escorted Sam's friends off the property and then came back for Sam, who was strumming his guitar and singing to himself.

"Has someone killed the cat?"

"You'll have to eat those words, when we get to Number One."

"Come on, it's bedtime, even for superstars."

"It won't be long, you know."

"Bed," said his dad wearily.

"We're almost ready."

"Bed!"

"The question is . . ." said Sam, with perfect seriousness, "is the world ready for us?"

A couple of days later, after a lot more practice, Sam decided they were ready to record. Jamie wasn't concentrating because he was thinking, not for the first time, how much better things would be if he was the manager. He kept missing his cue.

"Cut! Cut, cut!" Sam told him. Jamie jumped on the button.

"That's it. Now play it back. Louder. Turn it up."

Jamie rewound the tape and then turned the volume up almost to full. They all put down their instruments and listened.

Luke was desperate to laugh; Kat looked as if she was in pain; Jamie kept shaking his head, but Sam just smiled. He knew it was important to keep everyone's spirits up. That was his role as a leader: to make sure the troops didn't get discouraged. By the time the recording ended the troops were in despair.

Sam jumped up and turned to skin palms with

Luke. "Yeah! Great stuff. Fantastic! We've got a real winner there."

"Have you been listening to the same tape as us?" asked Jamie.

"It was a good start," said Sam.

"It was the living end," said Jamie.

"It *was* pretty gruesome," agreed Luke.

"A bit more practice and we'll be awesome."

"But we haven't got any more time. The tape's gotta be in by Friday," Luke reminded him. "We've got to post it tomorrow."

"You can't post that," said Jamie.

Sam looked thoughtful. "Just leave it to me. I'll handle it. It's all in the editing," he said, knowledgeably.

Jamie snorted. "They'll bust a gut, when they hear that . . . that . . ." He was lost for a suitable insult.

"What do you know about it? You're just the flipping roadie. You'd think you were the flipping manager." Jamie blushed, thinking Sam had been reading his mind. "When I want your opinion I'll ask for it."

"That's it," said Jamie. "I'm off. I'm sick of you throwing your weight around." And he turned to Kat. "You staying?" Kat was torn for a moment and looked to Sam to see if they were finished.

"Oh, you go with lover-boy," he said.

Kat picked up her drumsticks and glared at Sam. She wasn't prepared to waste her breath on him.

"Same time tomorrow, Flea Brains," said Sam; no one was amused.

"Drop dead, Cow-pat," muttered Jamie.

After Kat and Jamie had left there was an awkward silence in the shed. Luke looked at Sam reproachfully.

"What's up with you?" said Sam.

"It's you. You're getting to be a bit of a bully."

"*You're* getting to be a bit of a girl. Like Jacko with his curly hair and his earring."

Luke frowned. Sam had always been jealous of Jamie's stud. His dad wouldn't let him have one.

"I warned you what'd happen if we let girls in."

Luke couldn't bear Sam to get started on that one. He tried to lighten things with one of their old games.

"You have been warned! Girls can seriously damage your health!"

"I'd rather be tied up with a tarantula," said Sam, grinning.

"I'd rather eat curried cockroaches," said Luke.

"I'd rather eat meatballs full of maggots."

"I'd rather sleep with slugs."

Sam felt reassured. He'd been starting to think Luke was going soft on him.

Neither of the boys noticed the door open a crack and a girl's head appear.

"I'd rather have a bath full of bugs."

Luke turned the sweeping brush into a guitar and danced around with it. Looking up he spotted Chloe Fisher.

"So this is where you hang out," she said.

"I never heard you knock," said Sam rudely.

"Sorry to intrude," she said, withdrawing.

Luke just wanted the floor to open and swallow him whole. Chloe Fisher was the last person he wanted to be making a complete idiot of himself in front of. He and Sam exchanged looks and, without a word, headed outside after her.

CHAPTER THIRTEEN

The Vice Squad were in Sam's yard. Victoria was over at the house, talking to his mum.

Sam marched up to them. The girls looked Sam up and down.

"Nice outfit," said Zoe.

"Been to a funeral?" said Chloe.

Sam was not amused. "What're you lot doing here?"

"We might be starting riding lessons," said Serafina. "Victoria's talking to your mum."

Chloe smiled at Luke and Luke grinned back. He was as pink as a bar of rock. Even Sam couldn't miss it. "Are you after him?"

111

Chloe smiled noncommittally; Luke turned away, embarrassed.

"Come on," said Sam. "Let's get back."

"Are you practising your band?" asked Zoe.

"Can we come and listen?" asked Serafina.

"No, you can't," said Sam.

"Why not?" said Chloe.

"You might put us off," said Luke, shyly.

"We won't," she promised, smiling shyly back.

Sam gave them a despairing look.

"We're still interested in being in it," said Zoe.

"We'll think about it," said Luke.

"We won't," said Sam.

"Victoria says you're probably rubbish, anyway."

"*Smash Hits* obviously don't think so," he told the girls, self-importantly.

"What d'you mean?"

"We made a demo tape. And they think it's brilliant."

There was a strange noise from Luke; he sounded as if he was gargling.

"Wow!" said the girls. "Honest?"

Sam smiled patronizingly at them. "So we'll be getting real dancers, not little girls."

Zoe ignored the insult. "You could try us."

The girls turned to join Victoria who was shouting to them.

"Give us an audition," Chloe called over her shoulder.

"OK," said Luke.

"Forget it," said Sam.

The moment the girls were out of earshot, Luke rounded on him. "What did you tell them that for? We haven't even sent the tape off yet."

"So?"

"We might not get picked."

"'Course we will," said Sam, with supreme confidence.

"But what if we don't?" Luke was desperate.

"We will. Anyway, what does it matter?"

"We'll look so stupid."

"In front of Fishface, you mean. That's why you're so keen on having girls in the band. I know what's going on."

"Oh, rack off," said Luke. He watched the girls cross the paddock to look at the horses.

"Do you honestly fancy *her*?"

Luke shrugged.

"Have you ever kissed her?"

"'Course not!" Luke didn't like this conversation. He tried to ignore Sam, but Sam was not easily ignored.

"I'm going to tell her," he said and set off at a run.

"Tell her what!" Luke, terrified, felt obliged to follow.

Victoria was giving her friends the benefit of her knowledge of horses and everything to do with horse-riding. The three girls, only barely listening, were collecting armfuls of newly-mown grass into a huge heap and jumping into the middle of it, squealing.

As Sam came closer to the girls, Luke caught up with him and tried to restrain him.

"Don't," he begged. But Sam brushed him aside. "What're you going to say?"

"Just leave it to me."

But even Sam was thrown off course by Victoria's greeting.

"What do you pair of gonks want?"

"Shut up, you. This is my place. I live here, you know."

"Get lost," said Victoria. "I've talked to your mum. I don't need to talk to her donkey."

"Oh, Victoria," said Chloe.

"Yeah," said Serafina. "It is his place, you know."

Victoria pulled a face and got down from the fence. "I thought you were practising your famous band."

"We are. When you lot have finished snooping around."

"Fireballs From Hell! More like Damp Squibs!"

"Just get lost," said Sam.

"Anyway," said Chloe, "we're not snooping around."

"We've got better things to do," said Victoria.

"Yeah, like this," said Zoe. She grabbed a huge handful of grass cuttings and stuffed it down Luke's T-shirt. All three girls turned on Luke and pelted him with grass. Then they set on Sam. Sam's sweatshirt was a tighter fit but the girls managed to get some inside.

"Aw, man. These are my best clothes."

"Ahhh, what a shame!" They covered the boys with more grass.

Luke and Sam looked at one another, then skinned palms.

"Die!" they said and turned on the girls. In seconds they fled, pursued by the boys who grabbed them one by one and rolled them in grass. They fell like skittles and lay there squealing. With three down and one to go, the boys turned

115

to face Victoria. She stood before them looking like a cross between Margaret Thatcher and Cruella De Ville. She held out her plaster as a warning. The boys faltered.

"Don't dare," she breathed. "Don't even think about it."

The boys looked at one another and burst out laughing. They turned and fled back to the shed, screaming, "Oh, help! Save us." They raced inside and slammed the door shut.

Both boys were in a state of high excitement. They grabbed their guitars. Sam switched on his cassette player and turned up the volume until it was almost deafening. The boys mimed and sang along with Meat Loaf, their voices filling the shed.

For a moment they were both convinced they'd got through to the final. In their imagination they could see the TV cameras, they could hear the screaming fans, they could *feel* the adulation. They knew they were the greatest.

Across the field, the girls got up and brushed off the grass. They were feeling pretty excited too, despite Victoria's disapproving face. When the pounding music reached their ears, they looked over to the shed, surprised, amazed, disbelieving.

"Is that them?" said Zoe.

"Didn't I tell you?" said Chloe, smugly.

"There's no way that's coming from those two gonks," said Victoria.

"I bet it's their demo tape," said Serafina.

"No way!"

"Honestly. They just told us. They're in that competition."

"Sounds like the real thing," said Zoe.

"It's great," agreed Chloe.

Victoria listened again. Was it possible? Perhaps those trolls weren't as stupid as they looked.

Just then her dad drove into the yard and pipped his horn. The girls ran over and got into the car. As they drove out of the yard they wound down the windows.

"What a terrible din," said her dad.

"We know the band," said Chloe proudly. "They're in our class."

"Well, they sound almost professional," he conceded. "But it's still a din."

The girls raised their eyebrows pityingly.

"I wish they'd let us join," Chloe said to Zoe.

"You're not joining without me," Victoria warned them.

The girls looked uncomfortable.

"They won't let us, anyway," said Zoe.

"Sam won't," said Chloe.

"Don't worry about him. *He'll* let us," said Victoria, a plan beginning to form in her mind. "I know a few things about Sam Woollman. You leave him to me. We're as good as in that band already."

CHAPTER FOURTEEN

There was uproar in the classroom. Mrs Carter-Coombes had brought in her dog; her famous dog, a small yappy little mongrel called Bernard. It didn't look like an animal of unusual capabilities, but a dog is a dog and it was causing great excitement in the class.

"Ahhh. So sweet," cooed some of the girls.

"Can I take it for a walk?" asked Jody Poole.

"No, Jody, you can sit down and get on with your work. And Bernard is a *him* not an *it*. Perhaps at breaktime someone would be kind enough to take him out to answer the call of nature."

"What's that, Miss?" Billy Brewer knew full

well, he just wanted to hear Mrs Carter-Coombes say it.

"Get on with your story, Billy Brewer," said the teacher.

The band sat round their table. Sam tapped the precious tape on the table-top as he talked. The label read: *Fireballs from Hell – Demo Tape*, and the date.

Jamie was still irritated with Sam, but it wasn't a new feeling. "I thought you were supposed to have sent that tape off by now?"

"What tape?" said Sam, vaguely. "Oh, this is just a copy. Don't worry, I've sent it off." Luke looked horrified. "Sounds dead professional now."

"How come?" said Luke.

"I played around with it a bit. Fine tuning, you know."

Luke didn't know, he hadn't the vaguest idea what Sam was talking about.

"Well, that's the last you'll hear of that," said Jamie.

"We'll get a call, you'll see."

"We'd better," said Luke. He was feeling anxious now that the previous night's hysteria had worn off. "He's only told the Vice Squad we've already got through to the final," he told Jamie.

Jamie looked at Sam. "You did what?"

"It's cool. Don't worry. It'll happen."

Sometimes Luke couldn't make him out. He would have liked a fraction of Sam's self-confidence.

"You are off your trolley," was Jamie's opinion.

Sam ignored Jamie and turned back to his story. "I'm going to call this 'The Ghost Band'." Sam did most of his thinking aloud.

He began to write:

It was dead spooky in the shed. Dead quiet and spooky."

"I don't believe in ghosts," said Kat. "It's rubbish."

"I've seen one," said Jamie. "I saw Gismo's ghost." Gismo was Jamie's hamster that died. "It was curled up in a corner. It looked like a pair of socks."

"Probably was a pair of socks," said Luke.

"I thought I saw the Grim Reaper once," said Sam.

Luke hated to be the odd one out. "I saw a ghost in our bathroom," he said.

"What was it doing?" asked Jamie.

"Having a bath, of course." Then he spoilt it by laughing.

"Luke Harman, get on with your work," called the teacher. "Any more hilarity from your table and I shall have to think seriously about splitting you up."

"Limb from limb," whispered Jamie.

When Luke next looked up he found Chloe smiling in his direction. He wondered who she was smiling at, until he realized it was him! He dared himself to smile back, but Sam looked up and caught him.

"What're you grinning about, Hormone? You look a right dweeb."

"Just had a wicked idea for a story," he said, getting his head down and starting to write. But after that Luke couldn't keep his eyes away from the girls' table. Every time Chloe paused to think she looked over and smiled at him.

Luke could hardly keep his face under control. Terrified he might give himself away, he closed his eyes took a deep breath and let it out v-e-r-y slowly. When he opened his eyes Luke found the other three staring at him as if he'd gone mad.

"That must be some idea," said Sam.

"Either that, or he's constipated," said Jamie.

★   ★   ★

Victoria came into school late. She'd been at the hospital, having her plaster removed. It was sitting on her desk like a souvenir. Now, with the teacher's permission, she was walking around the classroom with a small box hung on a piece of string round her neck. She stopped at Sam's table.

"We'll have two Magnums and two Strawberry Splits," he said.

"Oh, very humorous," said Victoria. "I'm collecting for the hospital appeal, actually."

"Horse appeal, more like," said Sam. Victoria looked at Sam with contempt. "If that was a joke, it was in very poor taste."

"I wouldn't give *her* a penny," said Sam, when she was out of earshot. "You can't trust girls."

Kat let out a 'humph' next to him.

"Not you," said Sam, hastily.

Jamie looked at Luke and the meaning of the look was clear – say something, say something now! But Luke didn't.

"How's your bum, Hormone?" Jamie glared at him.

"You leave my bum out of this," said Luke.

Sam and Kat exchanged looks; they wondered what was going on.

"Charming," said Sam.

"Boys!" said Kat

In the dinner queue the boys found themselves next to the Vice Squad. Victoria wasn't there. She'd been given the dubious honour of taking Bernard to answer the call of nature.

"Is that your demo tape?" Chloe asked.

"Yeah," said Sam, jiggling it, nonchalantly.

"Can we listen to it?"

Sam shrugged. "Sometime."

Luke started to grin; Sam turned on him. "What are you looking so pleased about, Hormone?"

Luke exploded into glorious technicolour. "Me? Nothing."

As they started to move forward, Victoria pushed into the queue. "That dog," she said. "It's a menace. It kept trying to bite me. I took it all the way to the bottom of the field for it to do its *business*. I had to wait ages for it to perform and then when I got back, Catacombs made me go all the way back, with a *bag*!"

"What sort of bag?" asked Jamie.

"A *plastic* bag," snarled Victoria.

"What for?" asked Sam, trying a Billy Brewer.

Victoria turned away. "How can anyone be that thick and survive?"

Sam made rude signs behind Victoria's back. Jamie disappeared but in no time returned with a Post-it, which he stuck on Victoria's sweatshirt. The boys burst out laughing.

Victoria spun round. "What are you up to?"

Then the Vice Squad erupted too. Victoria spun round again and half the dinner queue joined in.

Unfortunately, the dinner lady soon put a stop to the fun, but the damage was done. *Pooper Scooper* was just the latest addition to Victoria's long list of nicknames.

But Victoria, like Sam, never stayed squashed for long. Later, on her way to the library, she dropped a note on Sam's table. Sam flicked it across to Jamie, as if it was a hand-grenade, and Jamie lobbed it at Luke. They batted it about between them as if it might explode at any moment until Kat grabbed it.

"You're like infants," she said. She started to open it.

"Hey, that's mine. Give it here." Sam read it out loud: "Meet me after school, behind the PE shed. I've got a prop–" Sam stumbled over the word. "She's got a what?"

"Proposition," said Kat, reading over his shoulder.

"She's got a plan, Dumbo," said Jamie.

"She's probably after you," said Luke.

"Don't even joke about it," he warned the other two, who were fluttering their eyelashes and drawing hearts in the air. "And *you*," he added, nodding at Kat, whose knuckles were half-way down her throat in an attempt to stop herself laughing, "had better cool it, if you want to stay on this table."

She did her best, but the idea of Sam Woollman and Victoria Topping going out together had to be the funniest thing she'd heard in ages.

Just before home-time Mrs Carter-Coombes began to shriek across the classroom, "I don't believe it! *Who* would do such a thing? Don't anyone move. No one leave the room . . ."

"Miss Marples," Jamie whispered to Luke.

From under her desk, the teacher produced a new improved Bernard. The small, but highly intelligent, white and brown dog was covered with large green spots. The class exploded into laughter. Mrs Carter-Coombes surveyed the room and spotted Sam. Sam shook his head and raised his hands as if surrendering. But fortunately for Sam her eye soon fell on Billy, who, for once, was sitting quietly in his seat. He had painted both his hands green all over. His neighbour was shaking her head. "You're weird," she said. When Billy opened his mouth to reply he revealed a whole set of green teeth.

Mrs Carter-Coombes descended on him, and keeping him at arm's length, led Billy to the Head's office.

Luke shook his head. "Bananas."

Jamie nodded. "Off the wall."

"Close thing," breathed Sam. And in the chaos this created, he made a quick getaway. Sam would never have admitted, even on pain of death, to being *frightened* of Pooper Scooper, but there was no way he was meeting her on his own behind the PE shed. No way!

CHAPTER FIFTEEN

The next morning, Sam sat at breakfast looking through his dad's camcorder. His sisters danced in front of it, pulling faces and generally showing off.

"Get lost. I want to film something interesting."

"I'm interesting," said Kirsty. "Look at me."

"It's not a wildlife film I'm making."

"Sit down and eat your breakfast," their mum told them. "Does your dad know you've got that?"

"I'm only practising."

Sam peered through the viewfinder and scanned the room. He panned round to the door and through it walked his dad.

"Oh, hi, Dad. Is it OK if . . .?"

His dad relieved Sam of the camera. "No. It certainly isn't."

"I just wanted to video the band."

"I'm sick of hearing about that band. I'll believe it when I see it."

"Just give him a chance." Sam's mum took the camera off her husband and handed him a cup of tea instead. "When you're ready, I'll come and film you," she promised Sam.

He got up and hugged her, making her blush. "You're ace, Mum."

"He can wrap you round his little finger."

"It's called charm, Dad." Sam lifted his dad's cap and turned it back to front. "Some of us have got it and some of us haven't."

"Some of us are going to need it. Have you seen the time?"

Sam leapt up from the table and out of the house, grabbing his swimming bag as he went. "See you, fans."

When Sam got to school it was wet so they were allowed inside before the bell. The band sat at their table reading comics. The Vice Squad were sitting next to the heaters, quietly brushing one another's hair. Zoe and Chloe were measuring each other's ponytail, while Serafina, armed with a pair of scissors, snipped off small locks of each girl's hair.

She sidled up to Luke. "Do you want to buy Chloe's hair?"

Luke coloured up and kept his eyes on his comic.

"All of it?" said Sam.

"No, silly, a lock of it."

"How much?" asked Jamie.

"Twenty p. It's for the hospital appeal."

"You must think we're stupid," said Sam.

But Luke reached out and snatched it off her. "I'll pay you tomorrow."

"You're barmy, you are," Sam told him.

"Do you want Zoe's?" she asked Jamie, holding up another lock.

Jamie looked like someone accused of a crime of which he was completely innocent. "No, I flipping-well don't. Why would I?"

Serafina shrugged. "Do you want some of Victoria's, Spam?"

Sam narrowed his eyes. "Now, why would I want a piece of Pooper Scooper's mangy wig?"

"Suit yourself." She held up a much larger lock than the one Luke had taken. Jamie grabbed it. "He'll pay you tomorrow," he said and waved it under Sam's nose, grinning.

The boys found a variety of uses for Victoria's lock of hair, including matching Hitler moustaches, a toupee for the class hamster and a pair of Denis Healey eyebrows, before Mrs Carter-Coombes arrived in the classroom and put an end to their fun.

"The bus is here. Line up for swimming," she bellowed above the noise.

As they got into line, Victoria, who was first as usual, smiled sweetly at Sam. "I'll save you a seat."

"Don't bother," said Sam, ungraciously.

"She's after something," said Jamie.

Sam dreaded to think it might be him.

The swimming baths were at the local High School. The class was divided into three groups: the largest group, the real swimmers, in the deep end with the swimming teacher, Mrs Gledhill; the few non-swimmers in the shallow end with Mrs Carter-Coombes, and a group of 'nearly swimmers', including Jamie and Sam, hovering in the middle with Mrs Tulliver.

Mrs Tulliver was pretty easy-going so they spent most of the lesson hugging the side, blowing bubbles and discussing their forthcoming leap to fame. Sam leant back in the water, imagining himself in his private pool with its built-in jacuzzi. He closed his eyes and for a moment felt the Hollywood sun beating down on his face.

"Shark alert! Shark alert!" Jamie tried to warn Sam, but a determined hand had already gripped hold of Sam's wrist.

"I need a boy volunteer," Victoria told Mrs Tulliver. "I'm just borrowing Sam."

In the deep end, the real swimmers were getting into pairs to try life-saving. Victoria, short of a partner, dragged Sam away.

"Get off! I'm not in your group." Sam tried to fight her off, but it was like being caught by an octopus.

Victoria gripped him tighter and towed him into the deep end. Sam was terrified. He couldn't bear being in such close physical contact with Victoria Topping. But, far more pressing, he was well out of his depth. Sam was sure he would drown.

"Just lean back and listen," Victoria ordered him. She clutched him by the chin and forced his head back in the water.

She's going to kill me, thought Sam. Just when he was about to hit the big time. It would be another of those tragic stories of talented young lives cut short: Buddy Holly, James Dean, River Phoenix, Sam Woollman . . .

Victoria bellowed in his ear, "I know what I'm doing. Relax!"

Relax! He'd have felt more relaxed with a black widow spider round his neck. The water splashed over Sam's face. I'm too young to die, he thought, fighting to get his head up.

"I'm supposed to stun you if you keep on struggling."

He'd stun *her* if he ever got out of here alive. She'd have her arm back in plaster, Sam wanted to tell her, but his mouth was full of water.

Victoria took advantage of this situation and started to lay out her 'proposition'. Sam, head back in the water, listened. He didn't have a lot of choice.

Back in his own depth, Sam looked like someone who had survived a near-death experience. Jamie tried not to laugh.

"You saw her. She tried to drown me."

"She's definitely after you."

"Worse than that," said Sam, bleakly. "Much worse."

Luke joined them, followed by Victoria and the Vice Squad, swimming in formation, like a team of synchronized swimmers.

Victoria bobbed up, looking very smug. "So, that's arranged."

"What's arranged?" said Jamie.

"We're going to be dancers for your band."

The girls leapt out of the water and cheered. "Excellent!"

Luke felt like leaping up with excitement too, but he restrained himself.

Jamie turned to Sam in amazement. "How come?"

But Victoria answered for him. "Let's just say I made Sam a proposition he couldn't refuse."

Back in the changing room the two boys confronted Sam.

"What happened?"

"What did she say to you?"

"Just lay off, you pair." Sam already felt as if he'd been mugged.

"You said, no more girls."

"You said, over my dead body."

"It almost was," said Sam, shivering every time he thought about it. "It almost was."

★　　　★　　　★

134

During the afternoon, Luke got up from the table to change his paint water, which looked like thick sludge. At the sink he felt a hand on his arm. It was Chloe's. She slipped a note into his hand and walked away.

Cool as a cucumber, was the phrase that leapt into his mind. He stayed there running water for five minutes before he dared go back to his table. The note, in his jeans pocket, sat there like an unexploded bomb for the rest of the afternoon.

At home-time, Victoria marched up to Sam's desk. "What time shall we come tonight?"

"Not tonight," said Sam. "Tomorrow, maybe. I'll let you know."

"We need to get started," Victoria insisted.

Sam struggled to get back in charge. "You can't come tonight. I've gotta go out . . . I've gotta stay in . . . I'm washing my hair."

Victoria walked away, disappointed.

"Don't ring us. We'll ring you," he muttered.

"What did she say to you this morning?" asked Luke.

"Nothing," said Sam, but his friends looked distinctly unconvinced.

"I just thought, let 'em join if they want to."

"I don't get it," said Jamie.

"Look, Idiot Features, you're the one who wanted them in the first place."

"Well, I think it's a big mistake," said Kat.

"Why've you changed sides?" said Luke.

"I don't trust Victoria Topping."

Neither did Sam, but Victoria had got him where she wanted him and there was nothing he could do about it. He would never forgive his mum for this. She'd delivered him into the hands of the enemy. Just wait till he got home.

CHAPTER SIXTEEN

Sam hit his house like a tornado. He took the stairs two at a time, shouting, "Mum! Mum! How could you do it?"

She found him ransacking the photo album, surrounded by piles of loose snapshots, desperately searching for one in particular.

"It's not here. I can't find it. Oh, Mum, you haven't. You wouldn't. You couldn't . . ."

"Sam, what's going on?"

"You've been talking about me, to Victoria Topping."

"About you?"

"Telling her things. About me, when I was little."

"What sort of things?"

"Embarrassing things. You know. About me . . . in the chip shop . . . weeing . . . on the floor . . . everybody watching."

Sam's mum burst out laughing. "Oh, that."

"*And* running down the road with no nappy and a bare bottom. And *other things*. You told her everything."

"Why does it matter? You were only a baby."

"*And* you gave her *that* photo."

"Which photo?"

"The one showing my backside. You gave it to Pooper Snooper."

His mum coloured up, immediately giving herself away. "I only let her borrow it. She said it was cute."

"Cute? Cute! You know what this means, don't you. *You* have put me in her power for the rest of my life. This will hang like a dark cloud over my whole future."

"Oh, Sam, stop being so dramatic," she said, wandering off and leaving him surrounded by photos. "And you can clear up that mess before your dad comes in and finds it. I hope you haven't forgotten, no band tonight. We're going to see your granny."

Sam didn't reply. He was too deep in despair.

This must be what it was like for pop stars and other celebrities when secrets from their past were discovered by unscrupulous journalists, and their stories splashed across the Sunday papers. He could imagine it: *World-famous lead singer from the phenomenally successful Fireballs rock band exposed in bare-bottomed baby scandal. "He weed on the chip-shop floor!" said his fans in disgust. "How can we look up to him now?"*

Sam groaned to think how his friends would treat him if this got out. He couldn't afford to let that happen, not at any price.

"Sam," his mum called up. "Phone."

"If it's Pooper Snooper," he shouted back, "tell her I'm ill. Tell her I'm out. Tell her I've emigrated."

"Sam, come down this minute. It sounds important," his mum hissed at him, covering the mouthpiece. "It's a man from Mega Records. He says he wants to talk to you."

Luke took out the note from Chloe and read it again, for the fifteenth time. He read it out loud, to Con and Dom, but the two lizards were a disappointing audience. Luke already knew its contents by heart but he enjoyed the business of taking out the note, unfolding it and reading Chloe's small, neat handwriting.

Do you want to go out with me? I want to go out with you. If you want to go out with me, I'll go out with you. Tell me tomorrow. Don't tell anybody else. I ♡ you. Chloe.

Luke refolded the letter and then furtively kissed it, which made his hands begin to sweat. Luke had never kissed anyone, apart from his mum and dad. He realized he needed some practice. He kissed the letter again, small light kisses and then a big one which left a wet smudge on the paper. He blotted it on his jeans. Suddenly there was a heavy bang on the shed door. Luke thought his heart had stopped beating.

"Phone!" Lucy yelled. "For you."

Luke stuffed the note in his pocket and yanked open the door. "There's no need to yell," he yelled at her.

Lucy stared at him and once more Luke felt as if she could see inside his head.

"What've you been doing in there?"

"Nothing." Luke turned and put the lizards back in their tank.

"Why're you so red, then?"

"Get lost," said Luke.

Lucy followed him up the path. "Mum says you're up to something."

Luke turned to tell her to rack off, but the grin on Lucy's face was unnerving. "It's your girl-friend on the phone," she said. Luke's legs turned to lead. His sister followed him into the hall.

"You took your time," said his mum.

Luke approached the phone as if it might bite him. "Hello?" he said, tentatively. His heart was beating fast and he closed his eyes as he waited to hear Chloe's voice answer back.

"OK. Do you want the good news or the bad news?" Sam started up at the other end. Luke turned on Lucy, his face was murderous.

"It was a joke," she mouthed at him.

Luke felt so mad he couldn't help taking it out on Sam. "Don't start that," he snapped.

"Chill out, Hormone. What's the matter with you?"

"Just get on with it. I've got other things to do, you know."

"OK. OK. The bad news is we can't practise tonight, I've got to go to my granny's, yawn, yawn. But the good news is: Da . . . daaaa! I've just had a phone-call!"

141

"So?"

"From Mega Records!" Sam was so excited, Luke could visualize him bouncing up and down at the other end of the phone.

"Well? Say something," Sam yelled.

Luke was silent, speechless in fact. He waved his free arm in a puzzled gesture which was wasted on Sam. He simply couldn't believe it and yet his mind was racing with the possibilities.

"You mean, we've got through? We're going to make a record?"

"Well, probably," said Sam, coming down from the ceiling. "Anyway, the guy says he wants to talk to us. He wants to check out our potential . . . or credentials or something like that."

"So we haven't got through?" Luke wanted to know whether to get excited.

"As good as," said Sam. "Just go round and tell the others, will you?" And he put the phone down.

As Luke passed the kitchen door, he could see Lucy, hiding behind their mum. He gave her the slit-throat sign.

"You're dead," he mouthed at her. "You're dead."

CHAPTER SEVENTEEN

An hour later, Luke arrived at Jamie's house. It was a bit of a squeeze in Jamie's room because Kat and Blossom, Jamie's dog, were already in there and it was rather a small room.

"You're never going to believe this—" Luke burst in.

"Sit down and shut up," Jamie told him, irritated at the interruption. He'd been reading aloud from the screen and Kat and Blossom were obviously a more attentive audience than Con and Dom. Luke sat down next to Kat.

"So . . ." Jamie recapped, "Bert and Bonehead are tied up in this container. They've been at sea three days, nothing to eat or drink—"

"They'd be dead," Luke interrupted.

"I told you to shut up," said Jamie.

"You can't go three days without water."

"Well, they're dehydrated. They're weak and Bonehead's hallucinating but they're not dead, all right?"

"They'd be dead," Luke insisted.

"It doesn't matter," said Kat. "Carry on."

"Look, can this wait?" said Luke. "Sam's been on the phone."

"Big deal."

Luke paused for effect. "I think we've got through."

Jamie and Kat looked at him, mystified.

"The competition! Sam's had a phone-call from this guy at Mega Records. He wants to see us."

"He's having you on."

"Seriously."

"If you believe that, you'll believe anything. You heard that tape."

Jamie's certainty began to unnerve Luke.

"Yeah, well, Sam said he was going to play around with it. Perhaps he improved it."

"Yeah, and pigs might fly," said Jamie.

"Let's go and ask him," Kat suggested, getting up.

"We can't. He's gone to his gran's," said Luke. "I'm sure he's on the level."

"Why would he lie about it?" said Kat.

They all wanted to believe the good news and in the end the pull was too tempting to resist.

"Just think about it," said Luke, grinning. "*Top of the Pops*, here we come."

Kat started bouncing on the bed in excitement, making funny squeaking noises. Luke had never seen her so animated.

"I'm going to get a set of black leathers," she announced.

Luke and Jamie burst out laughing and soon they were all roaring with laughter so that Jamie's mum came in to see what all the noise was about.

"You three seem to be having a good time," she said. But now they all fell silent. They obviously didn't feel confident enough to share the news yet.

"Just a joke, Mum. You wouldn't get it."

"Well, if you're not going to Sam's tonight, you can take the dog for a walk."

"Later, Mum, later," said Jamie, turning back to his screen. "I'm glad we've got a night off," he said, after she'd gone. "I was getting bored, night after night."

Luke had been starting to share Jamie's opinion, but now the phone-call had come – and now that Chloe was going to be involved – it was all far from boring. He patted his jeans pocket. But then he remembered he'd left the letter in a safe place. A very safe place. Just thinking about it, though, gave him a giddy feeling. He stretched back on the bed and smiled at his reflection in Jamie's mirror.

"I wouldn't call being a teenage superstar *boring*," he said.

Kat elbowed him in the ribs. "You poser."

Luke grinned and elbowed her back. "I know," he said. It was the second time that day he'd been touched by a girl. Luke thought he could get to like it.

Jamie looked at the two of them giggling and rolled his eyes.

"OK, you pair of truffles," he said, "if you calm down, I'll read you the rest of my story."

"Oh, great," said Luke, looking sideways at Kat. "We were really hoping you'd say that."

Kat smiled back. She was getting to like Luke. He was a good laugh.

As Luke rounded the corner of his street, he could see his sister's head poking out of her bedroom window. What was she after, he wondered?

When she saw him, Lucy waved what he took to be a white hanky.

"Hi, Lukey," she called. "Look what I've got." She waved it again and suddenly Luke knew it was not a hanky she was waving.

"You little termite," he shouted up to her. "I'm going to tear you limb from limb."

The hand, holding the precious letter, disappeared from view. The window slammed shut. Luke was so angry he had to restrain himself from smashing his fist against the side of the house.

He lay in bed awake for hours. This time it wasn't thoughts of Chloe that were keeping him from sleep. He was trying to concoct a suitable revenge for The Worst Sister in the Entire History of the World.

CHAPTER EIGHTEEN

Sam slid into his place as the morning music came through the speakers. It was a fast Irish reel and the whole class suddenly sat up, bouncing in their seats and clapping their hands.

Mrs Carter-Coombes banged on her desk with a ruler. "That'll be quite enough, thank you. Music is to listen to. We use our *ears* for listening, not our *bottoms*. *Bottoms* are for sitting on."

Most people slumped back on theirs, but Sam sat up grinning at the rest of the band, *I told you so*, written all over his face.

"Is it for real," said Jamie, "about the competition, or have you been telling porky pies?"

"You can ask my mum. This fella, Sandy

O'Flaherty or something, rang my house yesterday after school."

"And?"

"He said we sounded *amazingly professional*. But he wants to see us."

"What for?"

"Probably wants to see what we look like."

"He's got the photos."

Sam looked sheepish. "I didn't send the photos. They were rubbish."

"They were not," said Luke.

"They were rubbish," agreed Jamie.

"So when's he coming?"

"I dunno." Sam didn't like being questioned. He was getting really irritable. "He didn't say. He's gonna drop in and surprise us."

Jamie kept shaking his head. "There's gotta be a catch. It was *our* tape you sent?"

Sam's face went very red. He snatched his books off the table. "Right, that's it! Just because you've got no confidence in us." He got up and stormed across the classroom. Luke was worried. When Sam got in a razz like that, it usually meant he'd got something to hide.

Sam found a place to sit on his own, next to the fish-tank. He hoped that by depriving the others of his company, he'd teach them all a lesson.

Unfortunately his plan backfired because he then found himself pestered to death by Victoria and the Vice Squad. They'd heard the news and were very excited about it.

Victoria showed him sketches of herself dressed up like Madonna. "What do you think, Sam? Which do you like?"

"I dunno," he said, pushing her away. "You decide."

Sam was as uncomfortable with this new, eager-to-please Victoria as he was with the old bossy version.

He finally got rid of them and sat, head in hands, watching the fish swimming round and round without a care in the world. Right now Sam would have liked to swop places with them. The truth was he was in a bit of a spot. He'd taken a few chances and he wasn't at all sure that he was going to get away with them. But Sam was never one to brood. He started to feel bored so he went back to sit with his friends. He decided he'd punished them enough.

During breaktime Luke told them about his sister stealing Chloe's letter. Luke never could keep a secret. They were all amazed.

"You . . . and Fishcake? You're seriously deranged," was Jamie's opinion. Kat tended to agree, but as usual kept it to herself.

"Why did you leave the letter where she could find it, Pea Brain?" said Sam.

Luke was indignant. "I told you, I bugged the box."

"Oh, big deal. I bet she was really wetting herself. A bulb *and* a buzzer. Scary!"

"She's got no right to go into my things."

"Well, that's girls for you," said Sam. He was about to launch into his favourite subject when he spotted Victoria and her friends heading towards him. He ducked behind the mobiles and made for the boys' toilets. But back in the classroom there was no avoiding Victoria.

"Look, are we going to have a practice tonight?"

Sam tried to stay cool. "Listen, Victoria, we're not quite ready yet. I mean, you lot have got to get your act together and we're still . . . a little bit rough round the edges."

Jamie almost burst out laughing. That is some kind of understatement, he thought to himself.

"Oh, don't be so modest. We heard the tape. Even my dad said it sounded almost professional."

Her dad? What was she talking about? Luke shook his head; there was something that didn't add up here.

"Exactly when did you hear this tape?" asked Jamie.

"The other night when we were over at Sam's."

"I didn't see you there."

"After the grass fight," said Chloe. "It sounded great."

Jamie was still puzzled but the penny had dropped for Luke; he closed his eyes. Then Sam realized too.

"And we've been practising like mad," Victoria assured him. "We'll show you tonight."

"In our gear," said Chloe, grinning.

Sam tried to speak but his brain seemed to have been disconnected. It was like the swimming pool all over again; he felt completely out of his depth.

"Six o'clock tonight, then?" said Victoria, clinching the deal.

Sam nodded, and snarled, "All right."

When the teacher looked up from her desk, the sight of Victoria Topping teaming up with Sam Woollman made her nervous. She couldn't imagine what those two could have in common but whatever it was she was sure it needed discouraging. She moved in and broke up the little gathering.

Jamie and Kat waited for some explanation, but Sam wouldn't speak. It was left to Luke to explain that what Victoria's dad had thought sounded *almost* professional was actually Meat Loaf, with his Number One hit.

"You pair of prats," said Jamie.

"It wasn't our fault," said Luke. "We didn't do anything."

"Not half," said Jamie.

Luke was really worried. "What's going to happen?" he asked Sam.

"Look, we have a slight problem." Sam tried to play things down. "It's nothing we can't handle. We'll sort it."

But none of the others felt reassured. They couldn't wait for lunchtime.

The moment the lesson finished the band headed outside to find a bit of space to have an emergency meeting. Straightaway bickering broke out.

"You've blown it this time," said Jamie.

"I warned you what'd happen," said Sam, "if girls got involved."

"That's got nothing to do with it."

"Oh, no? Well, perhaps *Mastermind* contestant can tell me why the trouble only started when Lulu's sweetheart and her gruesome friends tried muscling in on *my* band."

"*Your* band? How come it's always *your* band?"

"Pack it in," said Luke, almost having to hold the two boys apart. "Chill out, the pair of you."

Kat tried to calm things down too. "I don't see the problem. *They* might've heard the wrong tape but this man from Mega Records hasn't, has he?"

Sam didn't reply. He started grinning. He looked quite pink with embarrassment.

Luke began to feel uncomfortable. "What have you done?"

Jamie almost shrieked, "I knew it. I knew there was a catch. That wasn't our tape you sent, was it?"

Sam kept on grinning, but said nothing.

Kat wanted to strangle him. "Tell us," she hissed at him.

"OK! It was Meat Loaf, more or less, I roughed it up a bit."

"What d'you mean, roughed it up a bit?"

"I added a few background sounds, so they wouldn't know. I was only trying to buy us some time. We just needed more practice."

"You screwball," said Luke.

"You brainless idiot," said Jamie.

"I wasn't to know they'd ring back so soon."

"That's it. Count me out," said Jamie.

"Yeah, forget it," said Luke.

Kat was shaking her head in disbelief.

"Come on. It's no big deal. We just need a—"

"If you say list I'll stuff it down your throat," said Jamie.

"Plan," said Sam.

"Miracle," said Kat.

"I suppose this is when you find out who your friends really are. You make a little mistake—"

"*Little?*" shrieked Luke.

Sam, when desperate, usually played the emotional card. "I thought we were in this together. How many years have we been mates?" Luke began to look miserable; even Jamie couldn't meet Sam's gaze. "So now you're going to dob me in. Hand me over to the Vice Squad. Great friends you are."

"What do you want us to do?" Luke yelled. "The girls are coming tonight, expecting us to sound like Meat Loaf. And what if this Andy O'Flattery decides to show up as well?"

"Don't bother about him," said Sam. "It's the Vice Squad I'm worried about."

Kat still couldn't fully understand the problem. "Why don't you just tell them?" The boys all turned to her. "Tell them it was a mistake. That the tape they heard *was* Meat Loaf."

They looked at her pityingly. "Just forget it," said Sam, as if addressing a small child. "That is *not* an option. If you think we're going to make ourselves look idiots in front of that gang of gargoyles . . . Man, we'd never hear the end of it."

Sam was thinking more about his own fate if Victoria decided to let all his skeletons out of the cupboard. However, the other two boys agreed with him. The prospect of being the butt of Victoria Topping's cruel jokes felt like a fate worse than death.

"Anyway," said Sam, taking charge again, "it's perfectly clear what we've got to do." The others waited for his words of wisdom. "We'll just have to mime."

"Now you have finally flipped."

"We'll never get away with it," said Luke.

"'Course we will. They do it on the telly all the time," said Sam, finally bouncing back. "Be there at half past five. I'll take care of everything. Just trust me."

CHAPTER NINETEEN

Sam's mum had been in favour of Sam's band while it kept him happy and out of trouble, but now that he was careering round the house trailing a huge pair of velvet curtains in his wake, plus extension leads, a couple of spotlights and a ball of string, she wasn't so sure.

His sisters, wearing floaty white nighties, followed him, getting under his feet and making nuisances of themselves.

"We want to be in Sam's band," they chorused.

"Will you keep these insects out of my way?"

"Don't call them that," his mum warned.

Sam could think of far worse things to call

them, but sensibly he kept these to himself.

By five o'clock he'd made all the preparations he could. He stood back and surveyed the scene. Well, he thought, that's it. He was within reach of success. It held out its hand to him temptingly. The question was: would he be allowed to grasp it. Or would it be snatched away, leaving him falling headlong into a deep humiliating hole? Well, he'd soon know the answer.

Unlike Sam, Luke was not sitting at home contemplating his fate. He was sitting in a tree in his garden, waiting for the fireworks to go off.

Lucy had come in ten minutes ago and found all her soft toys missing. Her three teddies, two dolls and the rest of her stuffed animals. Luke could hear her voice getting shriller and shriller.

"M-u-m? Have you been tidying my room? Where's Luke? What's he done with my toys? *I HATE HIM!*"

At last Lucy came out of the back door and headed for the shed. She hammered on the door and yelled, "Luke, open up. Let me in. Have you got my teddies in there?"

She rattled the latch but then noticed that the padlock was in place. From his perch above her,

Luke could see Lucy furrowing her brow. He could imagine the primitive machine that was Lucy's brain slowly cranking itself up to produce an idea. He was afraid he might laugh out loud and give himself away, or worse, lose his balance, fall out of the tree and land on her head.

Lucy was too short to see through the window, so she dragged over her dad's wheelbarrow, climbed into it and peered inside the shed.

Luke held his breath and waited. The screams, when they came, were pure magic. She jumped up and down in the wheelbarrow and banged on the shed. She threw back her head and yelled as if her lungs would burst, "M-u-u-u-m!"

Luke hugged himself. He couldn't wait to tell the others.

Jamie was trying to think about other things too. He couldn't bear what a shambles it all was and how embarrassing it was going to be when this man showed up. He put it firmly out of his mind and tried to pick up his story where he'd left off.

But this put him in a bad mood too, because he knew Luke was right: Bert and Bonehead probably would have died by now, without anything to eat or drink. Oh, rats! he cursed under his breath. There was too much going on in his head: this business with the Vice Squad, the unbelievable stupidity of Sam sending off a fake tape and now Luke and Chloe Fisher. He'd no idea Luke was even interested in girls. Not in *that* way.

It had started Jamie worrying about yesterday when Serafina had offered him some of Zoe's hair. Why had she offered it to *him*? Did she think . . .? Did Zoe think . . .?

Jamie felt hot and embarrassed. That was something else he didn't want to think about. It wasn't that Jamie didn't like girls; he got on with them fine. But he didn't want to go out with one. "Absolutely *not*." He shook his head, as if to convince himself. He put his attention back on his screen. Bonehead! That was a stupid name for a start. What Bert needed was a more interesting assistant, more intelligent and . . . beautiful. That's what Bert needed.

Jamie typed in:

Bert looked down at his beautiful, devoted assistant Zoe . . .

Honestly! He must have her on the brain. He deleted the name quickly and typed in Natasha. That was more like it.

Natasha was unconscious, getting weaker by the

hour. Bert knew he needed help soon or she'd die. Bert had to come up with an idea . . .

It was a pity Bert Lurch-Hooter wasn't in the band. He'd have got them out of this stupid situation, thought Jamie.

Of course, *he'd* never have got them into it in the first place.

Kat was thinking about the band; she couldn't think about anything else. She sat in front of the television seething. She kept asking herself, how had she got involved with these crazy boys in this crazy situation?

She knew that the sensible thing was to drop out of the band. But for some reason she couldn't. She didn't want to let them down. She knew, if she did, they'd say it was because she was a girl. She could hear Sam now, "I told you. You can't rely on *girls*." Well, she'd show him she was as reliable as any boy.

Kat dreaded to think what complete fools of themselves they were likely to make, bound to make. She let out a heartfelt groan.

"Are you all right, Sweetheart?" her mum asked, suddenly concerned.

"No, I'm definitely not all right. In fact I'm mad. I must be. Stark staring mad."

"I don't think so. A bit eccentric, perhaps."

"Mad," said Kat.

"Is there anything I can do?"

"No. It's too late for that," said Kat, gloomily. And she buried her head in her hands and wished it was all over.

CHAPTER TWENTY

When Luke and Jamie arrived, they helped Sam finish rigging up a couple of extra spotlights. Sam hoped that by cleverly angling them to cast large areas of shadow, they'd have a better chance of fooling the girls that they were really playing. What Sam hadn't worked out was what they would do if the man from Mega Records ever turned up; *he* wouldn't be so easily fooled. But Sam preferred not to dwell on that one.

The boys were all feeling so nervous they couldn't stop talking. Every time Luke tried to tell the others his sweet story of revenge, they kept interrupting him.

"So I hung them all, by their ears, over the rats' cages—"

"What for?" asked Jamie.

"Just wait and listen, will you?"

"Why didn't you put them inside?" said Sam.

"Aw, man, they'd have eaten them. Her Sindy was only on top of Templeton's cage for a minute and he chewed most of its hair off. She nearly passed out when she saw it."

"I'm not surprised," said Jamie.

"They just needed the rat slobber wiping off. *They stink! They stink!* she started up."

Jamie and Sam exchanged looks and started coughing.

"I don't smell. I had a shower before I came out."

"Yeah, and we all know why." Sam grinned at Jamie. "He's getting himself worked up to it. He's gonna kiss her tonight."

Jamie watched Luke writhing with embarrassment. "Hormone? He wouldn't know how."

"I suppose you would," said Luke. "I suppose you're very experienced."

"Well, I don't call chests *you-know-whats*."

"Chests! Chests!" snorted Sam. "Chests are what you keep blankets in. You mean breasts, don't you?"

164

Jamie and Luke turned the colour of postboxes. What if anyone walked in? What if Sam's dad heard them?

"You pair of earmuffs. You know nothing about sex."

Luke and Jamie couldn't deny it. Luke always got sent to bed if there was any hint of sex on television. Jamie spent all his time in front of a computer; there was no kissing on computers.

"So, how come you know so much?" Luke asked Sam.

"He doesn't. He doesn't know any more than us."

This seemed unlikely to Luke, who could have written what he knew on the back of a bus ticket. Sam smiled his inscrutable smile and Luke didn't know who to believe.

Suddenly Kat appeared in the shed, which silenced the boys. This kind of conversation was OK in front of each other but definitely not in front of a girl!

"You're late," said Sam, accusingly.

"Sorry," said Kat.

"Perhaps we can get started now. We can at least have a run-through before you-know-who comes. Right, now pay attention. This is the plan."

*   *   *

While Sam was briefing the rest of the band, a shiny new Range Rover turned into the drive. It wasn't a vehicle Sam's dad recognized; he came out to see who it belonged to. The man who got out was wearing an expensive-looking leather jacket. He took out a piece of paper and checked the address.

"I'm looking for Sam Woollman," he said.

Sam's dad narrowed his eyes. "For what?"

"I bet you're his dad." The man introduced himself. "I'm Sandy O'Flaherty from Mega Records. I understand he has a band."

Sam's dad didn't confirm this, but he didn't deny it either.

"Over here," he said. He led the young man towards the shed. "Does he know you're coming?"

"Ermm, not exactly. I thought I'd just surprise him, you know."

"I think you'll do that all right."

"Only he sent us this tape. It was very good. A bit too good, we thought. How old's Sam?"

The two men grinned at one another. Sam's dad had a feeling there were a few surprises in store and not just for Sam.

* * *

The atmosphere in the shed bordered on hysteria. Sam's attempts to calm the others, by pretending to be completely laid back himself, were having the opposite effect.

"So, I give Jamie the nod, he slips behind the curtain, turns on the cassette, we all start miming. Couldn't be easier."

Jamie groaned. "This is crazy. They won't be fooled for a minute."

"We'll never get away with it."

"It's so stupid."

Jamie pleaded once more for sanity. "Let's just forget it, OK?"

"Look, it's what they do on *Top of the Pops* all the time."

"To their own records though," Luke pointed out. "Not other people's."

"What's the difference? It's all miming. It's dead easy."

Sam showed them how easy it was with a short mime of his own. Unfortunately with no music in the background it just made him look very silly. "You see?" he said. "It's a breeze."

"You fat poser," said Jamie. "Do you know how stupid you look?"

"Rack off, you little pile of rabbit droppings."

Sam was sick of Jamie's interference. The two boys flew at each other.

"For goodness sake," said Luke, who was feeling terrified already. "We haven't got time for this." He dragged them apart just as the door opened.

"You've got a visitor," Sam's dad announced.

None of the boys moved or made a sound. They looked like three rabbits, caught in the headlamps of a car. Kat hid behind her drums.

"Sandy O'Flaherty," the man introduced himself. He held out his hand hoping that Sam would identify himself. But the boys just stood there watching the man's head nodding. It was a kind of nervous habit, but it mesmerized them.

"He's come to hear you play," said Sam's dad pointedly.

"Sorry if it's a bit of a surprise," the talent scout apologized. "I can see it's made you nervous."

This was such an understatement there was no suitable reply.

"Great set-up you've got here," he continued, starting to feel nervous himself. His head nodded even more. "It's got a good feel. Good vibes. Guitars and drums . . . nice simple line-up, nothing wrong with that. So, erm, about this *tape* you sent us . . ."

This time the silence descended like a lead balloon. It flattened them all, even Sam. This felt like his worst nightmare scenario. But there was worse to come.

In the silence that continued, they heard the sound of car doors and then running footsteps and giggling voices.

"Here comes trouble," Jamie whispered.

Sam's dad stood back against the wall, arms folded, smiling. They all watched the shed door, expecting it to burst open. But there was just a timid knock, then Chloe's head peeped round it.

"Close your eyes. I think you're in for a surprise."

Sam groaned inwardly. "Come in and get on with it," he snarled.

The three girls threw back the doors and made their entrance. "Da, daaaaaa!" They stood in a huddle, hands on their hips and did a little twirl. They tried to look sophisticated but spoilt the effect by immediately starting to giggle.

But behind them was an apparition.

The apparition didn't smile and it certainly didn't giggle. It looked deadly serious and seriously deadly. Victoria was dressed entirely in black. She wore black tights and a short black skirt and masses of black eye make-up. But the most amazing thing, certainly in Luke's opinion, was that she was wearing a black bra over the top of her clothes. She looked . . . unrecognizable.

"Well?" she said. "What do you think?"

The band looked her up and down and then down and up.

"I said you were in for a surprise," said Chloe.

As far as Jamie was concerned, *surprise* didn't begin to describe it. Sam's confidence began to falter. He was back in the deep end and floundering.

Sandy O'Flaherty, on the other hand, began to relax. It was clear he'd wandered into some kind of mistake but, whatever it was, he suspected he was going to enjoy it.

"She is something else," he said to Sam's dad.

Victoria spun round. She hadn't seen Sam's dad or this trendy-looking stranger, partly hidden behind the door.

"Hi, there. I'm Sandy O'Flaherty, from Mega Records," he explained. "*Smash Hits* passed on the tape and I'm here to sort of . . . check it out, for authenticity, you know."

Jamie and Luke shot Sam a look, but it went unnoticed.

Victoria put out her hand. "Pleased to meet you."

"I'm looking forward to catching your act, when you're all ready," he said, nodding and smiling.

"Well, we're not ready actually. We need to have a run-through. Couldn't you come back in half an hour?"

"Oh, don't worry, I'll just hang around here . . ."

But Sam's dad came to the rescue. "D'you fancy a beer? While they get warmed up."

"Sure. Sounds like a great idea," the talent scout nodded.

When they left, the band heaved a collective sigh of relief before rounding on Sam.

"What've you got us into?" Jamie yelled.

"What're we gonna do?" Luke looked almost in tears.

Before Sam could respond Victoria took charge. "What do you think we're going to do? We're going to have a run-through, Dummies," she said. "Now, let's get going."

CHAPTER TWENTY-ONE

Fear always made Luke want to laugh. He knew it wasn't an appropriate response, so he disguised it as a coughing fit.

"What's the matter with him?" Victoria asked.

"Allergies," said Jamie.

"He's allergic to girls," said Sam. "Especially in fancy dress."

Victoria tried to look superior, but it wasn't easy in that outfit. "Just get yourself organized, before Sandy comes back." When Victoria was feeling nervous, it made her even more bossy. As soon as she looked around her, she wanted to change everything. "Do we really need this curtain? It's taking up too much room."

"That's my mum's curtain," said Sam. "You can't move that."

"We'll have to move these drums, then. We need plenty of room if we're going to be dancing."

Kat stood aside with her arms folded, wearing a mutinous look, while her drum kit was moved three times before it met with Victoria's approval.

In the background, the other girls were practising one of their dances. They sang to accompany themselves and Luke couldn't keep his eyes off them. He really envied their confidence. The way they moved with such ease was a mystery to him.

When the girls reached the end of their routine and noticed him watching them, he was surprised to see them go pink. It made them look a bit shy, and younger somehow. Luke sometimes wished he'd been born a girl, but he would never have said so.

For the moment, he'd managed to forget the trouble they were in; he was in his own world. But Victoria soon snapped him out of it. "You two stand over there." She pointed to a small space at the back.

"Stop bossing everybody around," Sam complained.

Victoria turned to Sam and a look passed

between them. To Sam it was as clear as if it had been written in neon: Chip-shop floor? Bare bottom down the High Street? Need I say more?

"It's not every day you get an audition with Mega Records!" she reminded him. "Let's get started, shall we? *Rat in a Trap?*"

"Can't play it," he said, sulkily.

Chloe was disappointed. "Oh, that's our best one."

"We could learn it," said Luke, helpfully.

"No, we couldn't."

"*Let's Get Closer*, then?"

"Nope," said Sam.

They went through a whole list of titles each of which Sam rejected. Either he couldn't or wouldn't play them.

Victoria was ready to blow a fuse. "*Bat Out of Hell*, then!"

Sam was about to deny they could play that until he remembered it was the number the girls had heard on the fake demo tape.

"OK," he said. "Just give us time to tune up."

"I thought you'd done all that!" she said through clenched teeth.

"These need fine tuning. You don't get to be this good playing naff instruments, you know.

174

We're not some rubbish outfit . . ." Sam rambled on, evidently playing for time.

Jamie and Luke closed their eyes as if in pain.

Victoria was getting suspicious. She looked down her nose at the boys. "You can play those guitars, I suppose? They're not just for decoration?"

Sam was struck by what a strong resemblance she bore to Brookside, the horse that bit her.

"Yes, we can play them," he snarled, tightening the string until it almost snapped.

Victoria stamped her foot. "We can't wait any longer!"

"I'm ready," he shouted.

Sam took up his place and Luke reluctantly joined him. Sam nodded to Jamie, who lowered himself from the workbench and quietly slid behind the curtain.

The girls assembled. Victoria stood, feet apart, with one hand outstretched in front of her as if she was trying to stop an oncoming train. The other girls copied her and attempted to keep their faces straight with varying degrees of success.

Sam rolled his eyes at Luke. "What *do* they look like?"

But Luke didn't respond; he was too scared. Kat sat, shoulders hunched, like someone under sentence of death. For the first time, looking at them all, Sam could see the funny side of it. He was tempted to throw his hands in the air and shout, "Joke! Joke! It was all a joke."

But one glance at Victoria killed that impulse.

The moment Sam heard the click of the recorder he gabbled, "One, two, one two three."

The music began to build up until it filled the shed. The girls, concentrating so hard on making a good impression, hardly paid enough attention to notice it. For one glorious minute Sam thought they might actually get away with it. He threw himself into his mime, strumming his guitar and shaking his head in time to the music.

He *looked* like a pop idol. He *felt* like a pop idol. His dream was finally coming true. Sam Woollman – Superstar! Yeah!

But Sam's dream was about to turn into a nightmare.

The door opened and in came two figures, slightly flushed from drinking beer.

Sam knew this was their moment of truth. He knew they couldn't keep it up, but he didn't dare stop either.

Victoria knew this was their big chance. They couldn't afford to put a foot wrong but Chloe, Zoe and Serafina already had. She halted mid-twirl and put up her hand. "Stop. Stop!" The girls collapsed in a heap.

But Sam pretended he hadn't heard and Luke followed his lead. Kat kept her head down. Jamie, behind the curtain, hadn't a clue what was going on.

"I said, STOP! We've gone wrong," yelled Victoria.

Jamie was in complete panic. In desperation he turned the music off. But the band went on miming without it.

Sam's determination to keep up the act drove him to more and more outrageous behaviour and Luke simply couldn't compete. He let out a whimper and looked pleadingly at Sam, to get them out of it, but Sam, by now, had gone into orbit. Kat sank lower and lower until she almost disappeared behind her drums.

The girls watched horrified. They couldn't believe what was happening.

The adult audience was almost crying with laughter.

But Victoria did *not* see the funny side of it. She started to scream. "What's going on? Where's that Jamie Jackson?" She took hold of the curtain and dragged it aside revealing a red-faced Jamie. The curtain fell heavily down on her and, as she staggered under the weight, she grabbed Sam. They landed in an untidy heap on the floor.

"Get off me," cried Victoria.

"Get her off me!" Sam yelled.

The other girls rushed to help her. As she got up Victoria stepped on Sam.

"Idiot," she snapped. "Nincompoop. Useless creature."

Victoria tried to restore her appearance but when she looked down she found the right cup of her Madonna bra had completely caved in. The boys were helpless; even her friends couldn't help laughing; but Victoria rose above it. Determined to distance herself from this fiasco, she grabbed her jacket and turned to Sandy O'Flaherty, who tried to keep his face straight.

"This was nothing to do with us, you know. We knew nothing about it. Honestly."

But no apology was needed. Sandy O'Flaherty had thoroughly enjoyed himself. His head nodded happily. "Well, guys, that was quite a performance. Nice try, but I should keep on practising." He turned to the girls. "But you were great. Real potential. Let's stay in touch. Couple of years and who knows." The girls squealed with excitement. "Thanks for a great time. I haven't laughed so much in years."

The two men went out to the yard and left them to it. Victoria rose to her full height. She turned to Sam and gave him a victorious smile. "No potential here," she said to the others.

"Let's go."

"Good-bye," said Chloe, without a backward glance. The door closed behind them.

Kat got up from her drums too. She'd had as much of these boys as she could handle. "That's it. I'm off," she said.

"What about the band?" said Luke lamely.

"What band? It was only ever something to talk about. That's all you lot ever do. Talk, talk, talk and I've heard enough."

She slammed the door, then put her head back in for a moment to warn them, "And don't anybody touch my drums!"

CHAPTER TWENTY-TWO

Alone at last the boys exploded. Jamie turned to Luke. "What did I tell you? I don't know why we ever listen to him. Him and his crazy ideas. Sometimes he talks out of his backside."

"We'd have been all right if *you'd* done your job right, you fossil-face," Sam yelled at him.

"What do you mean? If *you* had any brain cells at all you'd have known it was a duff idea in the first place."

"That's it. That is *it*!" said Sam stumbling across the shed to get at Jamie. He grabbed him by his sweatshirt.

Luke put down his guitar and waded in. "Pack it in, you pair of turkeys." He got between the two of them, but they immediately turned on him. Soon all three boys were rolling round the shed floor, thumping and blaming each other for everything that had gone wrong.

Before they were able to do too much damage, Sam's mum came through the door, with the baby on one hip and the camcorder in her free hand.

"Just stop that!" she said.

The boys sat up, looking so sorry for themselves that, beyond a disapproving face, she didn't have the heart to pursue it. They got up and started dusting themselves down.

"I'm sorry it took me so long," she told Sam. "I've been trying to get this little monster to sleep for nearly an hour. She just wouldn't settle. But I'm here now. You hold her, while I get set up." She passed the baby to Sam.

"Aw, mum, I don't want her." But Sam jiggled Ruby up and down and made her smile. "Anyway, it's too late now, they've gone."

"I can do you three."

"No, it's all over. Forget it. Here, you have Pudding back; I'll have the camera."

"I'll come next time you practise," she promised them.

"There won't be a next time. We're packing the band in."

She looked at the boys sympathetically. "That's a shame."

"It's cool," said Jamie.

"No sweat," said Luke.

"Is it Victoria? Has she been causing trouble?" Sam's mum clearly hadn't yet heard about the evening's fiasco. The boys grinned at one other, remembering Victoria's temper tantrum and the lop-sided bra.

"We don't care about *her*," said Sam. "Band's are for kids. We're into films these days. Movies." Sam pointed the camera at his mum and moved in for a close-up, which made the baby cry.

"Be careful with that. You're dad'll have a fit if you drop it."

"Don't worry, we're gonna buy one of our own," Sam announced.

The other two were surprised; it was the first they'd heard.

But Jamie's eyes lit up. "I'm gonna write the scripts."

Luke wasn't going to be left out. "I'll be Tom Cruise," he said, "the main attraction." Pop star, film star, he didn't mind which. They both got the girls.

"You poser," said Jamie.

"This'll be our studio," said Sam. He moved the camera round, taking in the whole shed. "Scene one. Take one. Action!!"

Luke and Jamie walked home together. It was already dark.

"My mum'll probably have the police out by now," said Jamie.

Luke remembered that *his* mum had grounded him earlier, but he'd sneaked out anyway. Now he had to go in and face her and his dad.

"Don't let's go home," he said. "Let's run away. Let's hitch-hike to South America. Let's just disappear."

"Are you serious?"

"No," said Luke. "Not really." But it had been a nice idea. He tried to hold on to the memory of Lucy's toys hanging by their ears only inches above the rats' cages, and his picture of Lucy jumping up and down in the wheelbarrow screaming. And he wouldn't have missed the final showdown in the shed either. He could see the funny side of things now: Victoria staggering about under the curtain and rolling around on the floor with Sam; Sandy O'Flaherty creased up laughing; watching Chloe dance, that had been the best. What if he was in trouble? It had been worth it. Well, perhaps.

"My dad can be really heavy-handed," he said.

Jamie gave Luke a sympathetic punch. Jamie's mum had never hit him in his life. He supposed that could be one advantage of not having a dad. He couldn't think of any others.

When they turned into Luke's street, they could see Pubic Enemy's bedroom window open and her head hanging out of it.

"Here he is," they heard her shout.

Luke made a rude sign up at Lucy.

"You're for it," she called to him. "Dad's waiting for you."

"One day," Luke said to Jamie, "she's going to hang too far out of that window and I want to be there to miss catching her."

Jamie smiled. He could see lots of advantages to not having a sister. "Maybe Sam's right about girls," he said.

Luke shook his head. "Most girls aren't like her, thank goodness."

Jamie gave Luke another sympathetic punch. "See you, Ear Wax."

"See you, Bum Fluff."

Luke hung around, watching Jamie walk down

the road. He called after him, "Can I come home with you?"

Jamie turned back. He smiled and gave Luke a crossed fingers sign.

Better get it over with, thought Luke, and went through his gate.

"He's coming!" he heard Lucy announce. There was the sound of racing feet down the stairs, the front door opened and his sister stood there waiting for him. "Come on in," she said.

Sam lay in bed talking into his torch-microphone.

"Now, firstly, Sam . . . I can call you Sam . . ." Sam asked himself, in a rich American accent. *"Is it true that you've been offered a billion dollars to go to Hollywood?"*

Sam smiled modestly. "I'm sorry, I can't talk about that yet."

"But is it true that Madonna's gonna be in your next film?"

Sam shrugged. "I'm thinking about it."

Sam's mum and dad, on their way to bed, paused outside Sam's door. Sam's dad shook his head and grinned.

"What do you feel when people call you 'The New Spielberg'"

Sam smiled. "I think I can live with that."

"What *is* he like?" his dad whispered.

"Come on," said his wife. "Leave him alone."

Sam called out, "Oh, Dad . . ."

"What?"

"Can I borrow your camcorder tomorrow?"

"Absolutely not."

"Aw, go on. Just till we get our own."

"Categorically, *no*!"

"He'll think about it," said his mum, going into the bathroom.

"Aw, thanks, Dad," said Sam. "You're the best."

"Oh, Margaret! Now look what you've started."

"It serves you right. You shouldn't wind him up," she said, closing the bathroom door.

Sam lay back. He looked across his bedroom to the canvas chair he'd brought up from the kitchen. Pinned to the back was a large sign. It read: Sam Woollman. DIRECTOR.

He could hear his dad outside the bathroom door, still complaining. "Didn't I tell you not to encourage him? Why does nobody in this house ever listen to me?"

Sam turned out his light. He closed his eyelids.

Behind them the action was set in motion, the cameras rolled.

"Cut!" he whispered.

The Girls' Gang

by Rose Impey

Everyone wants to be in a gang, so Sandra, Jane, Cheryl, Jo and Louise create one, just for girls of course! What's their goal? To get rid of the dreaded Ralph Raven, the most big-headed boy in the school!

Mr Mills and Year 6 are witnesses to the fierce battle that is waged between the Girls' Gang and the boys, and the combined efforts of five girls, the smelliest stink bomb in the world and a ghost called Claud guarantee entertainment, so watch out!

The Moon of Gomrath
Alan Garner

Had Colin and Susan known that the Moon of Gomrath is the time of year at which the Old Magic is most likely to be aroused, they would never have lit a fire on the Beacon, but when they find their blaze is giving off no heat, it is only the last in a line of eerie discoveries. For already Susan has suffered strangely at the hands of a black and formless evil in the old quarry, and rumour has it that the hideous Morrigan, too, has left her haunts in the bleak northern wastes to bring death and destruction to pleasanter lands.

As the elves and dwarfs come swiftly to the caves of Fundindelve, home of the wizard Cadellin Silverbrow, to seek council for the coming struggle, more fearsome forces are gathering in the woods on Alderley Edge, and they, too, are preparing for battle.

The powerful and enthralling sequel to *The Weirdstone of Brisingamen*.

Thursday's Child
Noel Streatfeild

When Margaret Thursday was a baby, she was found on the steps of a church with a note which said:

This is Margaret. Each year, fifty-two pounds will be sent for her keep and schooling.

Margaret finds a home with old Miss Sylvia and Miss Selina until she is ten, when suddenly there is no more money forthcoming. And because there is nowhere else for Margaret to go, the rector says, "The archdeacon has told me of an orphanage, an exceptionally pleasant place. They would take you for nothing."

Margaret gulps hard. "That's where I'll go. If I can't stay here, I'd rather go to a place where I am treated as a proper person."

But no one told Margaret, or even knew, about the horrible Matron of the orphanage...

Order Form

To order books direct from the publishers, just make a list of the titles you want and send it with your name and address to:

Dept 6,
HarperCollins Publishers Ltd,
Westerhill Road,
Bishopbriggs,
Glasgow G64 2QT

Please enclose a cheque or postal order to the value of the cover price, plus:

UK and BFPO: Add £1 for the first book, and 25p per copy for each additional book ordered.

Overseas and Eire: Add £2.95 service charge. Books will be sent by surface mail, but quotes for airmail despatch will be given on request.

A 24-hour telephone ordering service is available to Visa and Access card holders on 0141-772 2281.